Catch that Gremlin!

KD Greaves

www.kdgreaves.com

PLEASE SIR, THE GREMLIN
ATE MY HOMEWORK

K.D. GREAVES

D1332561

C158046634

Prologue

The car rolled on through the gloomy wetness of the Cornish countryside. Every mile was a mile further and further from London. Further and further from everything and everyone I knew. It was almost the end of May, but the rain fell in dull, heavy swooshes and sweeps. Like my mood really. Surely there were laws or something about banishing your twelve-year old son to a part of Cornwall that even the Beast of Bodmin Moor avoided?

Okay, I wasn't ever going to bring home a certificate saying *'Kade Jones, model student'* (Kade pronounced as in aid by the way) but I wasn't that bad either. Unfortunately, Dad didn't agree, which was why I was on my way to Uncle Fitz's. To a house with a wall built to keep things in instead of out. The house that hid our Family Secret. No wonder Uncle Fitz's brother and sister had done a runner years ago. I was being sent to the house of a *nutter*. And to school there too. Grosse Manor *and* Grosse High. The panic inside me shimmied up an octave. I knew that if I spoke my voice would come out in a high-pitched squeak.

I'd begged Dad to take me with him on his research job abroad. I'd *promised* him that I'd behave. But no. I was banished to the back of beyond. Didn't Dad read the letters that came from Grosse Manor? They were scary. Especially when they said things such as: **It's time for the boy to be prepared.** Ha. The rest of the world might be stupid enough to think Uncle Fitz was a saintly old man running a sanctuary for rare, endangered animals, but I wasn't fooled.

Now, you don't know Grosse Manor, but if this was a horror movie it was the bit when lightning strikes; thunder roars; the music goes **DAH, DAH, DAAH;** and the camera zooms in on whoever's about to meet a grisly end. In this case, *me!*

Chapter 1

$$(1) \ 17x + 12 = 54$$
$$(2) \ 6x - 16 = 5x$$
$$(3) \ 4x - 4 = 3x$$
$$(4) \ 7x - 12 + 3x$$
$$(5) \ 30 - x + 12 =$$

Please Sir, the Gremlin ate my homework!

"Please Sir, the Gremlin ate my homework." Stupid or what? I should've stuck with last week's excuse of the dog. I hated that Gremlin. If it was here, I knew it'd be laughing.

Mr Worthington stared down at me. I stared up at him. I could see the imprints left in his lower lip by his long, sharp teeth as he chewed over my latest excuse for not handing in my homework. At least I'd woken 7Y up. I could feel their hungry interest. Until now everyone'd been drooped zombified over their desks – a side effect of Mr Worthington's Maths lessons. Someone started up a drum roll on the table. Mr Worthington's top lip curled. Whatever followed wouldn't be good. I'd already crossed him at break when he'd caught me watching memes on my phone. (I had to have some fun or I'd go mad!)

"How dare you use your mobile in school!" he'd roared. "You know the rules! Give it here. Now!" Honestly, he was more like a cop than a teacher. From where I stood, I could see my phone lying on his desk. To my right, Jacob Lis grinned and drew a hand across his throat.

Mr Worthington put the tips of his bony fingers together and rested them on his chin. His disapproval rolled over me like dark, grey waves. "Kade Jones. In the month that you've been at Grosse High, how many detentions have I given you for not handing in homework?"

"A lot."

The class laughed. A furious glower from Mr Worthington cowed them into silence before pouncing back on me. "Are you trying to be funny?"

"N...no, Sir." It was true. I wasn't *that* stupid.

Mr Worthington continued staring. "You live at Grosse Manor, don't you? Sir Fitz Withershins is your uncle."

"He's more of a distant relative," I said. "A very, very distant relative." I'd enough problems without adding Uncle Fitz's questionable genes.

Mr Worthington's fingers drummed a slow rhythm on the tabletop. The beat sounded like a death march. "I believe your uncle owns a private zoo for endangered animals?"

"Yes, Sir."

"Litter duty at lunchtime. I'll be sending a letter home. Sit down." The words dripped acid. "If by Gremlin you mean that one of your uncle's pet monkeys or another beastie destroyed your homework, then say so. Don't waste my time with ridiculous stories. Class, open your books at page forty-four." He gave his attention to the Smart Board.

I trailed back to my seat, pretending I didn't care about the sniggers and pointing fingers. Sitting down, a sharp pain exploded in my left shoulder. I span round. A hostile glower met mine. Arjun Baiga who sat in the row behind had jabbed me with his ruler.

"Lucky he didn't believe you, isn't it, Kade?" he hissed.

My lip curled; that poke had really hurt. "What's it to you?" I hissed back.

Arjun's fists curled. He leant forward. "What's it to me? Duh! Unlike Mr Worthington, I *live* in Grosse Village, remember? *Everyone* there knows about the manor."

"Arjun! Kade!" The teacher's voice sliced the air. "Get on with your work!"

The words were delivered in such a terrifying tone that my heart leapt up and smacked into the back of my teeth. Arjun squeaked, seized his pen, and buried himself in his textbook. I tried to do the same, but what he'd said kept on dancing across the algebra questions. Everyone in Grosse Village knew about the manor. Uncle Fitz hadn't mentioned **that**. At least it explained why all the village kids avoided me. With my address, I'd avoid me. Snatching up a pencil, I stabbed it through the textbook. It wasn't fair. At my old school I'd had *friends*. For the rest of the day I nursed my already humongous grudge against Grosse Manor's inhabitants.

By home-time, my mood hadn't softened. Pushing through the crush of screaming kids fighting to reach the school buses, I rehearsed a snarky speech for Uncle Fitz about keeping secrets. But I'd barely run through the first sentence before the school gates loomed up. Grosse High was pocket sized compared with most secondaries; in fact, it had so few students that there was talk of it closing – YAY! The school shared a name with the village and Uncle Fitz's small, shabby manor, but was miles from either. Most of the students and all the staff lived elsewhere. The Grosse Village kids travelled in their own parent run minibus because where they lived was so remote that not even Sat Nav could find it. Me? I'd my own humiliating transport. Victor.

Victor was Uncle Fitz's ancient chauffeur who'd worked at Grosse Manor for like, well, *ever*. He reminded me of an escaped, unwrapped mummy circa Tutankhamen. Why he carried on working beat me. Or why he insisted on upsetting the school bus drivers by parking in their transport bays. Today, as usual, Victor was getting honked at. A driver leapt down from her bus and whacked an angry hand on the car's windscreen.

"Can't you read?" she bawled, gesticulating at the massive and impossible to miss, **NO VEHICLES EXCEPT SCHOOL BUSES** sign.

Pointless. Victor's deaf – real and selective. Even more embarrassing though, was how all the students were falling over, laughing. But not solely due to Victor's illegal parking. Uncle Fitz's car came with its own little quirks including an engine that sounded like a T-Rex with toothache! The car might once have been described as a classic limo, but now it had more in common with Victor. In other words, it could fall apart at any moment.

"Oy, Kade! Why's your car like a skeleton?" Arjun yelled. "They both rattle!"

The joke was pathetic, but even so everyone laughed. Broiling with shame, I tried to shrink deep inside my blazer and hide. Arjun, having scored his stupid point, sauntered off with his little band of cronies. This gave me a window for legging it over to the limo minus anymore wisecracks. I slunk into the back of the car, sinking down into the plush leather seat. Victor turned his creased, yellow face on me.

"Go. Quick," I hissed.

Victor wasn't a fan of quick. We trundled off in a way that made slow look fast. The village minibus rumbled by; Arjun and his gang pulled faces at me through the window. Leaning my head against the back of the limo's pull-down table, I gave in to misery. Why couldn't I be at my old school? Today was Thursday; all my mates would be at cricket practice.

"Nice day at school, Master Kade?" Victor's grey, gravelly voice shovelled into my thoughts. The old vulture knew the answer, but he enjoyed winding me up. I could see the malicious glint in his rheumy eyes as he squinted at me through the rear-view mirror.

"No," I said, checking my phone. Confiscated items had to be returned at home time. I'd hoped there'd be a message from my best friend, Arnie, but there wasn't. I took the disappointment out on Victor. "And you should be watching the road instead of me. Unless you're planning on adding sheep to the list of things you've recently run over."

Victor sucked in his wormy lips. Casting me an evil glower he took revenge by driving at one mile per hour.

By the time we'd crawled through Grosse Village (old and creepy) I'd lost the will to live. Any slower and we'd have stopped!

But not even Victor could drag the journey out forever. Eventually, having dragged through a maze of dusty and difficult, twisty lanes the car pootered to a halt outside Grosse Manor's ivy clogged gates. The ivy was deliberate, making the gates less noticeable to anyone passing by; although as the place was in the back of the back of beyond, who'd be passing by beat me. The gates were also electronically locked for added security. Victor faffed about searching for his gate fob. Still, this, plus his caterpillar slowness in inching the car up the long, winding driveway gave me time to complete my Maths homework before having to deal with the torture of another of his annoying habits. The Car Door Game. Victor was a bit of a control freak with the car. He wouldn't let anyone in or out without his permission. The one exception was outside the school gates. But only because that was when he played Dodge the Bus Drivers.

"Master Kade," Victor wheezed, rattling his way out and around. "We've arrived."

I ducked under his arm. In front of me, Grosse Manor showed itself off. With reason. It was impressive. At least from the outside. Inside was another story. Originally Tudor, but with Georgian and Victorian add-ons, it stood in its own park with an orchard, kitchen garden, a folly, lawns, woodland, flowerbeds and arbours. The house's double fronted oak doors opened onto a wide porch, pointing to a set of sweeping stone steps and an ornamental fountain with a swimming pool sized basin. The house and grounds had once been protected by a moat, but Uncle Fitz had drained and replaced this with a high wall that kept the manor hidden.

The wall hid other things too. Like the owner of the insane bark that now mangled the air. ***"WOOOFFF!"*** It was Uncle Fitz's dog, Me, Myself and I, eager for a meet n' greet. Over-friendly and built like a tank, the mutt had no understanding of personal space. His idea of hello resembled a mugging. Panic rising like high tide, I wrenched at the limo's door handle. But Victor had beaten me to it. *SNICK!* The locks clicked shut at the same time that the car's engine gurgled into life. I hammered on the window. Victor ignored me, driving off as Me, Myself and I's gargantuan form pounded around the corner of the house.

Taking one look at his dopey, let-me-kiss-you face, I legged it. A professional athlete couldn't have taken those steps faster. In seconds, I'd reached the front doors, the dog's feet ripping up the distance between us. *SLAM!* That was me kicking the doors shut. *WHAM!* That was him colliding into them. Unhappy whines and scratching followed as Me, Myself and I tried digging through solid oak. I left him to it.

Racing up the twisting staircase two steps at a time (speeds things up) I leapt off at the second-floor with no intention of stopping until I was safe inside my bedroom. Fortunately for me, Uncle Fitz's love of bare floorboards broken up only by the occasional rug, helped with this, and a zillion years of feet had polished the ancient wood to the slippery smoothness of an ice rink. I half ran, half skated across the landing, straight to my bedroom door. I was so practised by now that I could reach out ahead and twist the doorknob open without having to stop. Once inside, I dropped my schoolbag and collapsed on top of the large, springy bed, staring up at the ceiling, which was decorated with a yellow stain - the result of a bust water pipe. In shape, the stain formed an almost perfect outline of the Indian Ocean complete with a splat that could be Dad's boat. Dad was so sacked as a parent for moving us here. He'd called it 'making good life choices.' Mine, according to him, needed a few tweaks. Especially ones like the 'Throw the Washing Up Water Out of the Food Tech Window Challenge,' which I'd invented, and Arnie had helped showcase. How was I supposed to know that the Head Teacher was underneath? We were three floors up!

Following a very nasty discussion with Dad (Arnie escaped because I didn't grass on him), the Head said she was fed up with my behaviour and this was a final warning. Dad had gone *mental*. Half of London must've heard him. The words 'thoughtless', 'self-centred', and 'lazy' got a lot of airtime until he ended with, "Your mum would be so ashamed."

The attack had bitten deep. I'd had to fight myself not to cry. Dad knew I hated talking about Mum. All this because of a bit of *water*. In revenge, I'd dyed my hair seaweed green. Dad's response was to accept a three month project out in the Indian Ocean (he's a marine biologist which means that he likes fish without chips) and dump me in Cornwall. Usually, he took me with him on trips, but not this time. He said the Food Tech incident showed I was 'best kept far away from unsupervised access to H_2O'. Arnie said I could stay with him, but Dad sank that idea. As far as he was concerned, the water thing was as much Arnie's fault, except that *he'd* got away with it.

"Please let it drop; I've *said* I'm sorry," I begged, after Dad brought it up for the eighty millionth time. "Can't we move on?"

Wrong thing to say. I so need to choose my words more carefully. Dad took the 'moving on' bit literally. He said it was the most sensible idea I'd had in ages and rang Uncle Fitz. They had a long conversation in which my name came up a lot (not in a positive way from Dad's side) and I learnt two things. First, it's true that eavesdroppers don't hear good things about themselves; and second, we were moving to Grosse Manor for good! End of my life.

Dad would be back in two months when he'd finished researching some ugly fish that was supposed to be extinct. Until one of the stupid things let a fisherman catch it. Meanwhile, I was Joe Mateless. It's hard to make friends when you can't invite anyone home. This was because of Uncle Fitz's work. Rule number one and every other number too, was that the Family Secret stayed secret. So how did all of Grosse Village know about Uncle Fitz's bizarre and mad menagerie, headed by Lord Evil himself, the Gremlin? Uncle Fitz really did protect rare, endangered creatures, but not normal ones like tigers or gorillas. That'd be too easy. No, he collected Monsters. With a capital M. He'd even turned them into a proper noun! No wonder his brother and sister, the twins Clive and Hildegarde, never visited. Nobody knew where Clive was, but Hildegarde, an adventurer, lived in a Himalayan Monastery.

I banged my head on the pillow. I wanted to go home and hang with Arnie. His dad owned a café with a non-healthy eating policy, and I missed my free supply of deep-fried chips. *Deep-fried chips.* I lay there dreaming about processed food until the bedroom door crashed open. A ball of matted brown hair cannonballed across the floor. My worst nightmare. The Gremlin was out and about.

Coming to a stop by the side of the bed, the creature released an unpleasant cackle. It stayed there for a few seconds, quivering; thinking about its next move. Then, it bounced several metres into the air. *Slap*. It landed on my chest. Kaleidoscopic, septic-yellow eyes rolled their way into mine as the Gremlin flapped multiple limbs up and down like a deranged octopus. I froze. The Monster didn't have hands, but each shaggy, hairy tentacle had the speed and flexibility of a cobra, and its teeth, slapped into a brown, monkey face crossed with a frog (if you can imagine such a thing) were sharper than a coyote's. A bite from it was no joke.

Squawking, the Gremlin decided to play stop and search. It didn't mess about. Having located my phone, the squawk became a rumbling purr that quickly devolved into a batch of rich, fruity kissing noises. Bad sign. Kissing noises from the Gremlin had zero to do with affection. The only kiss that thing was into was the Kiss of Death. And armed robbery. In line with this, the Monster leapt up and scarpered, taking my phone as hostage.

"You thieving pickpocket!" I yelled, rolling off the bed. "Bring that back!"

Like that was going to happen! With a mocking hoot the Gremlin scampered up the staircase to the third floor, making a nifty turn via the chandelier. Swinging into the bathroom it settled on top of the toilet cistern, lifted the seat and held the phone over the bowl.

I froze in horror. "Don't you dare, you mutated, hairy squid!"

The Gremlin did dare. **_Splash!_** A tsunami of toilet water hit the floor. But the mangy Monster wasn't satisfied. It reached for the chain. Trapped in the whirling flush my phone sank like the Titanic. The Gremlin sniggered and flicked me a rude sign. My whole body sizzled with fury.

"You nasty little... Ooh!" I seized a bar of soap from the sink and lobbed it hard at the Monster. It dodged so I followed up with the nailbrush. This time I almost caught the toe-rag. With a screech, the Gremlin aerial cartwheeled out of the room. I followed, brandishing a towel.

"Kade!" Uncle Fitz stood on the landing the Gremlin curled up in his arms faking fear. He must've heard the racket and rightly guessed that, as with most things at the Manor, it more than likely had something to do with his Little Darling. Whatever, Uncle Fitz had appeared with suspicious speed. When necessary, he could move so fast you'd never know he had a false foot. He'd lost it on an expedition back in his zoological exploring days but had never explained how. It put an end to his exploring, but not, alas, to his Monster mania.

Uncle Fitz winced as I continued screaming insults. "Kade." Flicking back his thinning, grey hair, reproach radiated from him. "Dear me, what on earth have you done to the Gremlin?"

Me? I was the *victim*. The manky Monster, sensing victory, blew me a silent raspberry.

I clenched my teeth. "I haven't done anything! Creature Feature there's flushed my smartphone down the loo!"

Uncle Fitz's attention descended onto the nestling Gremlin sucking away on the tip of one of its tentacles, faking baby cuteness. It was an Oscar winning performance.

"Are you sure, Kade?" Uncle Fitz paused. "I'm, umm, I'm asking because you have always been rather negative about the poor dear."

"I... saw... it... pull...the... chain." I ground out each word through gritted teeth.

Uncle Fitz considered this. He knew the Gremlin had a long history of taking and breaking, but as usual he made excuses for his favourite. "It must have been an accident. The Gremlin wouldn't flush away your phone on purpose."

The foul fiend, mischief complete, slid out of Uncle Fitz's arms and snuck off towards the stairs. But it wasn't getting off that easily. Picking up the fallen soap, I took aim. Smack! The Gremlin squawked and fell flat on its ugly mug.

"I say," said a dismayed Uncle Fitz. "Don't do that, Kade. The Gremlin's extremely sensitive. You can squash its confidence very easily."

"You couldn't squash that thing with a sack of cement!" I snapped. "My *phone!*"

"I'll replace it," Uncle Fitz said hastily. "But for now..." He searched his immaculate, but at least forty years out of date, tweed suit. "I've something to discuss with you. It's time you brushed up on your Exotic Creature care skills. I've made a job list." The pocket patting continued, his hands fluttering over his clothes. My heart moved at the same pace. But from panic. Help with the Monsters? I'd rather swim with piranhas.

Mistaking the reason for my silence, Uncle Fitz patted my shoulder. "Don't take this badly, Kade; it's been a few years since you were last here, but your animal care skills are err... slightly rusty. Look at the misunderstanding with the Gremlin. Not that I'm blaming you. You're a good boy. Otherwise, I wouldn't be leaving you this marvellous place."

My heart, already at ground zero, slumped even lower. Soon it'd reach the earth's core. I wished that Uncle Fitz was horrible; it'd make it so much easier to say no. But he wasn't horrible. (Definitely nutty though!) To explain...

When I was five and Mum still around, I'd begged

Uncle Fitz to let me be the next him. Unfortunately, he never forgot it. It's another reason why I'm here. But, back to the conversation. Uncle Fitz eventually produced a folded piece of paper.

"I've made you a list of daily duties starting with the dog. He needs more exercise."

I took the piece of paper and scanned the spidery writing...

1. Walk Me, Myself and I twice a day.
2. Feed Old Smokey every evening.
3. Check that the Trolls haven't flooded their bathroom.
4. Makes sure Amelia is warm.
5. Keep an eye on the Gremlin.

"We'll scrap that last one," Uncle Fitz said hurriedly, guessing my thoughts. "The other jobs are enough for now and I'm sure you'll be splendid at them."

I glanced again at the list and then back at him. How should I put this? "Umm, Uncle Fitz, I'm not really into animals anymore..." I began.

"*What?*" Uncle Fitz's hair virtually leapt off his head, like I'd said the worst thing ever. "Why? Monsters are unique, truly exotic, and highly intelligent! For a start, mine all understand English, and some speak it too. How many other languages do you know?"

He had me there.

"Never mind." Uncle Fitz, his injured feelings forgotten, ruffled my hair. "We can't all have my Monsters' talents." He paused. "Listen Kade, I know what's behind all this."

15

He did? For a split second, hope sparkled. Until his next words snuffed it out.

"Yes, you're nervous about being up to the job. Perfectly understandable, but don't fret, I'll be guiding you until you're ready. Now, go and give Me, Myself and I a good run. He missed his afternoon walk as I was busy with some rather difficult business. We have a prowler hanging about. Yesterday, Glenda thought she saw someone by the potting shed."

(Glenda is Uncle Fitz's Housekeeper, although I've yet to spot her doing any actual housekeeper work. I think she's allergic to her job.)

"You could've told me this before," I said. "I've been leaving my window open."

I didn't want you to worry, but now it's becoming rather serious..." Uncle Fitz paused, his voice sober. "Have you heard any strange noises at night?"

"Yes."

"Where and when?" Uncle Fitz's eyebrows shot up.

"All the time. Everywhere. The Monsters are noisier than the entire animal population of Africa. They give a whole new meaning to the metaphor 'the place is a jungle.'"

"I don't mean the Monsters, Kade." Uncle Fitz shook his head. "A prowler could create big problems for us. We need to be vigilant. When you're walking the dog, have a look."

"For the mad prowler?" I said. "Really? Make it part of my pooch walk?"

Uncle Fitz thought for a moment. "Perhaps not. We don't want anything happening to our little doggy."

"That," I said, "isn't quite what I meant."

But Uncle Fitz had stopped listening. "I'll ask in the

village if anyone's heard anything." He pursed his lips, his tidy moustache dancing.

The mention of 'village' reminded me of Arjun. I folded my arms. "At school today, one of the village kids told me that they all know about the Monsters. You said nobody does and that's why I can't bring anyone here."

"I didn't mean the villagers, Kade. They have... *connections* to the Manor. You can bring home anyone from there. Had you forgotten?" Uncle Fitz looked puzzled. (Me too. What was he on about?) "When you lived here with your dad and..."

His words stopped mid-sentence. My mouth tightened like twisted rope. He'd been about to say the M word. An image of Mum holding the hand of a six-year old me surfaced. A snapshot of a long-ago day when I'd had two parents. Immediately, my brain dispatched a squadron of mind guards to seize and wrestle the picture back into the dungeon of locked up thoughts. Sucking in a deep breath, I fired a dark scowl at Uncle Fitz. But he looked so sad standing there, fiddling with his tie, that unusually, I found myself letting him off the hook.

"No, I don't remember. And it didn't feature in your letters. Monsters yes, village no."

"You know now," said Uncle Fitz, relieved that the difficult moment had passed.

"Wait," I said. "I want to know what the connection is between you and the village."

A melancholy moaning from the floor above, followed by a series of thumps and bangs hijacked the conversation.

"Oh dear," Uncle Fitz said. "I think the Gremlin may be visiting Amelia." Anxious to get upstairs, he hurried off, false foot clumping. "We'll discuss the village later."

Chapter 2

Dopey Dogs, Dangerous Dragons and Project Prowlers

In the hallway, Glenda was pretending to dust. (Really, she was playing games on her phone.) When she saw me, she made a half-hearted effort to move the duster over the library door. Each drag of the arm was accompanied by a heartrending sob – natural behaviour because Glenda's a Banshee. At least she was moaning quietly. On full volume she could take out an entire city! Glenda had elevated being grumpy to an art form. Uncle Fitz said it was her ex-fiancé's fault for dumping her at the altar two centuries ago.

The Banshee gave me a brief nod, shedding some of the zillion hairclips keeping her bride's veil in place. Glenda hadn't removed the veil since being ditched on her wedding day.

"Don't be going in there," she said, pointing a long finger at the library door. "The Gremlin's having one of its mad moments." From inside, crashes and bangs thunder stormed like an indoor fireworks display. Glenda tutted.

Curious, I poked my head around the door and saw the Gremlin cavorting from one piece of furniture to the next. Halfway through a back flip it realised it had an audience and changed course mid-air. Performing a triple arabesque across the rug the Monster thudded to a stop in the doorway, teeth bared. Glenda kicked the wedge free. The door slammed shut. Thumps and snarls vibrated through the wood. Unimpressed, the Banshee locked the door, pocketing the key. She stood there in silence for a moment, her green face rippling.

"I don't know what your dear uncle sees in that creature," she said in her lilting Irish accent, punctuated by a heavy pause whilst she pondered her next words. "At the moment, it's even worse than usual. It's as if something's upsetting it."

"No kidding," I said. "It flushed my phone down the loo."

Glenda twiddled her duster. "Your uncle believes we have a prowler, perhaps that's what's bothering it." She tapped me conspiratorially on the head with a bony finger. "I think I might have seen them. Yesterday, spying on me bringing in the washing. Then there's all the strange noises after dark. Poor Sir Fitz is up half the night checking the house and grounds. Haven't you heard anything?"

"No," I said. "I'm a heavy sleeper."

My lack of sympathy annoyed Glenda. She stretched up her long, thin body until I thought she'd go *ping*. "Get lost," she snapped. "You're holding up my dusting."

"I'm looking for the dog," I said. "Do you know where he is?"

Glenda stuck her nose in the air. "No." She slithered off, oozing huffiness.

I went to fetch the dog's lead. That bit was quick. Finding him wasn't. It took half an hour to track Me, Myself and I down to the pond where he lay watching the ducks swim about. They were ignoring him to the point of rudeness.

"Come away," I said, clipping on his three stranded lead. (Did I mention that he has three heads?) "They don't want to be your friend."

Me, Myself and I disagreed. He woofed a friendly goodbye to the ducks who carried on pretending he didn't exist and scrambled to his feet, sniffing my pockets for biscuits. That dog lives for three things: food, walks, sleep. Especially food. Uncle Fitz had found him abandoned in a cave in Greece, with a note tied around his middle neck. The note had said that he'd been dumped because he was a useless guard dog who ate too much and that whoever came across him could keep him.

Excited that it was walkie-time, Me, Myself and I pulled on the lead. Walking him is like walking three dogs. Each head spotted something different to chase and he made a strong but pointless effort to go in three directions. It took all my strength and cunning to bring him under control. The cunning bit consisted of dropping a biscuit on the ground. The mutt braked.

Head number one found the biscuit and crunched it up. Heads two and three whined.

"Don't be silly," I said. "You don't have three stomachs. You're one dog."

Hoping for more snacks, Me, Myself and I trotted by my side. His heads took turns to sniff the air, lick my hand and snap at passing flies. We walked through the courtyard, past the Japanese Flower Beds and over a lawn towards the back wall, hidden in this part of the garden by a small copse. The dog, who was obsessed with the area, now demanded to be set free: whining and scuffling about, claws raking up the grass. I let him off the lead. Barking, joyfully, he ran in circles, tail rotating like helicopter blades, and then bounded off, vanishing between the trees. Thirty seconds later a terrified howl shattered the air. Me, Myself and I blasted out, moving so fast his rear legs overtook his front ones.

"What's up?" I asked, as he cowered behind me, whimpering. "Meet a nasty bunny? A giant bee?" I studied the trees. They looked like trees should; green and ordinary. I nudged the dog with my foot. "Come on. Show me the problem."

He refused.

"Coward," I said. "There can't be anything in there that's a quarter your size."

Me, Myself and I lifted his upper lips in apologetic grins but remained glued to the grass. He gave me a look that said I could go and investigate if I liked but he was staying put.

"Big baby," I said. "There's nothing scary in there. I'll prove it. Now come on."

But the dog wasn't having it. He carried on pretending to be part of the lawn. I gave up.

To make my point, I strode straight to the exact spot where Me, Myself and I had raced out. Resting a hand against a tree trunk I peered inwards but could see nothing. The branches with their multitude of thick, green leaves formed a natural barrier. The only way to see beyond the leaves was to go in. Carefully so as to avoid scratching myself, I pushed back a couple of thin, springy branches and ducked into the copse coming out on the other side into a small, clearing. The only thing beyond this was the wall. It was all very summery and peaceful. The only sound came from the light breeze playing through the branches, making the leaves quietly whisper. I grinned. I'd been right. The dog was a big coward. He'd probably been frightened by a glimpse of his own shadow.

CRRRUNCH! SNICK!

From overhead a branch broke, it came thumping down, missing me by a fraction of a centimetre. Surprise and shock competed for first place. Either could have won. Especially given what came down with the branch. Clinging to it like a giant, hairless squirrel was a long, lanky figure wrapped in a camouflage jacket, face hidden by a rolled down steam-punk balaclava. Fear fizzed up inside me in hot acidic bubbles. I'd a horrible feeling that I'd found Uncle Fitz's prowler. I wanted to run, but my toes had curled themselves through my shoes and into the ground.

Whoever it was – man or woman; I couldn't tell – recovered before I did. Scrabbling to their feet they lunged forward, shoving me roughly out of their way and made for the wall. Bits of flint and gravel rained down as they clawed upwards. The wall had been designed in a manner that'd faze a professional rock climber, but this didn't slow their performance. Reaching the top, the figure threw one leg over and then paused, glaring down at me. Bad attitude oozed out from behind the balaclava. I'd like to say I played the hero, and went after them, but whoever it was, was much bigger than me and definitely out-skilled my climbing abilities. Instead I legged it. From now on, unless Uncle Fitz invested in a state-of-the-art security system, complete with electrified barbed wire, he could walk the dog himself!

On the grass, Me, Myself and I was still pretending to be a lawn ornament. He leapt up when he saw me hammering towards him, trying to pretend that he'd been on guard duty the whole time. The faker even gave a phony who-goes-there-bark. I didn't stop. I kept on pounding towards the house. The dog, panicked by my behaviour let loose a loud, terrified howl and shot off after me. We didn't stop until we'd reached the sanctuary of the kitchen. I slammed the door shut behind us, leaning on it, heaving for breath whilst trying to shove my heart and lungs back into place. Meanwhile, Me, Myself and I tunnelled into his elephant sized bed and hid shivering under the blankets. I stumbled past him, ears and head still fizzing. I had to find Uncle Fitz.

Unfortunately, he was otherwise occupied.

"No time to talk, Kade," he gasped, rushing past in the hallway, completely blind to my dishevelled and on the point of collapse state. "The Gremlin's playing dress-up with Glenda's best clothes. Need to rescue them before she finds out."

"But Uncle Fitz..." I wheezed. "The prowler... I... I've seen..."

"Later!" Uncle Fitz called, disappearing around a corner. "Tell me later. At dinner."

Collapsing against the wall, I slid down it, still taking deep gulps of air. Same as with the village! Uncle Fitz never had any time to listen when that Gremlin was about.

Eventually, having recovered enough to be able to walk normally, I wandered back to the kitchen. I still had my to-do list to complete. This was feed Old Smokey, Uncle Fitz's toothless and ancient Dragon, who lived in the specially extended and fire-proofed coal cellar. The problem was that I didn't know where Uncle Fitz kept the dragon food. I could hear Glenda rattling about in the utility room having switched from pretending to dust to pretending to do the laundry, so I went and asked her.

"In a bucket in the scullery sink." Glenda kicked a stray sock under the table.

Remembering that Glenda had seen the prowler too, I decided that this was a good opportunity to compare notes: see if our descriptions matched up.

"Glenda..." I began.

From out of nowhere, the Gremlin appeared. It cartwheeled into the laundry basket and started eating a towel. Glenda glanced down. I heard her hiss.

"Not on my wash," she sniffed. The next second she tipped the whole load, including the Gremlin, into the washing machine. I left her to it and went to collect Old Smokey's nosh. This proved to be a whole lot harder than it sounded.

Lifting the Dragon's bucket was like lifting weights. The pail was the size and weight of a baby elephant! In the end I dislodged it by levering it out with a frying pan. With a reluctant groan, the bucket grudgingly rose up and tumbled over the edge of the sink onto the tiled kitchen floor. Fortunately, it had one of those secured lids, so the contents didn't splatter everywhere. By the time I'd dragged the bucket to the door, my arms were longer than my legs. I'd no idea how skinny Uncle Fitz managed it every day. Or how he dodged Old Smokey's 'Feed Me' dance - a cross between a rock n' roll routine and needing to visit the loo.

The second he heard his dinner clanking up the Dragon was on the move. *Whisk!* Huge, scaly jaws jerked the food away. Old Smokey swallowed the contents in one gulp and then spat the bucket out over his head. It sailed through the air, landing with a dismal clang in a corner.

"Ha ha. Very clever," I said, smacking one of his huge shoulders. "Shift."

Old Smokey refused. Huffing and puffing he got in the way as much as he could. Despite Uncle Fitz having performed inter-dimensional feats with the cellar, the Dragon still took up a lot of space. Trying to push past him, I stood on his foot. This did **not** go down well. Old Smokey roared, threw up his knobbly head and smacked it on the ceiling, which upset him even more. He snorted out a short but intense stream of fire. Several random sparks attached themselves to my school shirt, turning me into a giant firework sparkler on legs. Howling, I slapped at the little glittering patches skipping up and down me. Uncle Fitz, who'd come to check on how I was doing, almost dropped his glass of water as I pranced past, tap dancing the length of the cellar corridor and back. He thoughtfully solved the sparkler problem by chucking the glass's contents over my shirt. I stood in front of him, all thoughts of the prowler forgotten as I smouldered in more ways than one. Instead of delivering dinner I'd almost become it!

"Problems?" he enquired.

"Problems?" I shot him an expression that was worthy of the Gremlin. "This," I rummaged in my pocket, yanked out the list and stuffed it under his nose. "This isn't a job list; it's a Death Wish!"

Uncle Fitz took the paper, which, as a result of the fire escapade followed by the water, was in danger of disintegrating.

"Perhaps," he said after a long pause, "I should ease

you into your duties. Let's leave it for tonight and pick up again tomorrow."

"By tomorrow I'll probably be dead," I said, snatching the list back. "It's not your Monsters that are endangered, it's me. I'm going to tell Dad."

It was an empty threat. Dad's boat was out of broadband range and unless Royal Mail employed mermaids as postal workers, writing wasn't an option either.

"Why don't you come and have some dinner?" Uncle Fitz suggested, attempting to distract me from anti-Monster thoughts. "It's your favourite. Curry."

I glanced down at my burnt shirt and nipped dead a last defiant spark. "Curry?" I said. "Really? Don't you think I'm hot enough already?"

But he knew how to tempt me. Curry's my favourite food. And Glenda, who'd been taught the art of Asian cooking by a Chudail (Indian equivalent of a Banshee), cooked it in a way that had you drooling for more. I caved in and let Uncle Fitz hurry me off to the dining room. On the way, I made a second attempt to tell him about the prowler.

"Uncle Fitz," I said, wiping soot from my shirt. "In the..."

The Gremlin zoomed past at a thousand miles per hour, bashing into the wall. It brought down several framed portraits before making a beeline for Me, Myself and I who'd chosen the wrong moment to wander in. With a rowdy cowboy yip the Gremlin bounced onto the dog's back, raised a long, curling tentacle and delivered a sharp slap to his rump. Startled, Me, Myself and I reared up and galloped off. Uncle Fitz gave chase, voicing futile pleas for the Gremlin to stop. I shook my head. Honestly, every time I tried telling anyone about the prowler the Gremlin distracted them. I ate dinner alone. Later, when I tried to find Uncle Fitz, Glenda said that he'd gone to visit a villager who needed help with their pet Boggart. By the time he returned I was asleep.

The next morning when I came down to breakfast, Uncle Fitz was sitting at the dining room table, drinking a cup of tea and reading a letter. Good. Whilst he was here and Gremlin-less, I'd tell him about the prowler.

"Uncle Fitz," I said.

Uncle Fitz jumped and hid the letter under the table.

"Bad news?" I asked, sliding onto a chair.

Uncle Fitz blushed. "No, no, not at all. A bit of junk mail. Nothing important."

"So why are you hiding it?"

Uncle Fitz went all flustered. "Err... spilt a bit of tea that's all. I'm using the letter to soak it up." This was about as believable as the Gremlin being Santa Claus. Why was he lying? I helped myself to a slice of toast. Whatever, Uncle Fitz wasn't going to tell.

"Uncle Fitz, listen," I said, "The..." I was about to say prowler, but Uncle Fitz thought I was still going on about the letter.

"Never mind the contents of my mail," he interrupted, pushing his specs further up his nose. "I've good news for you. It's about the friends thing. I popped in for a chat with my lawyer last night whilst I was in the village. Three of his children are coming to tea today. Two of them go to your school."

Putting down the butter knife, I eyed him suspiciously. "Who?"

Uncle Fitz poured another cup of tea. "The Simpkins. Joss and Calvin who are fourteen, and Ivy who's ten. There's Ben too, but he's older and away at college studying Robotic Mechanics; he's a very gifted inventor. Made an amazing GPS tagging device for the Gremlin, but the poor dear didn't like it. Possibly because it self-tasered the wearer if they tried to remove it. Mr Simpkins runs a small law office in the village and a bigger practice in Truro."

The word 'village' reminded me that Uncle Fitz still had some explaining to do.

"Yesterday, you said you'd explain about the village."

Uncle Fitz wiped his mouth on his napkin and helped himself to a crumpet. "Grosse Village," he said, spooning jam from a jar, "is very special. I'm sure you're familiar with the old cliché that fact is stranger than fiction?"

"Yes," I said, pointing at Glenda hip-hopping to the radio with the hoover.

"There's a link between the Manor and village," Uncle Fitz continued. "A *monstrous* link, so to speak."

"I hope that's figurative," I said. "And the villagers aren't mutants who morph into vampires or werewolves at night because I hate garlic and I can't afford silver bullets. Oh, I know, it's something worse. They're Gremlins so there's no way of getting rid of them."

Uncle Fitz laughed, which made me laugh too. Unlike Dad, Uncle Fitz totally gets me.

"No, Kade, they're not Gremlins and I've told you a hundred times that werewolves and vampires don't exist. The villagers are unique because they're either descended from or related by marriage to more 'human type' Monsters like... Glenda for example."

"Really?" I was amazed, although it explained Arjun's expertise in giving the evil eye. "Yes. The villagers understand my work and the need for secrecy. Any curiosity shown by outsiders to the Manor could bring the same to them, so we look out for each other. The villagers tip me off about exotic creatures needing help."

Chewing on a sausage, I thought about this. "So, Grosse Village is home to a load of anti-social Monster descendants? Interesting. Although also weird."

Uncle Fitz peered at me over the top of his glasses. "It might be better not to say that to them. Anyway, the Simpkins are coming to tea. Victor will collect Ivy from her primary school before collecting you and the twins."

I put down my fork. By the twins, Uncle Fitz could only mean the two brothers in 9J. Everybody knew them. Joss was Year 9 Sports Captain and Calvin was in charge of the Lower School Student Council. Calvin was so good at arguing that the Head always came away from the meetings outmanoeuvred and with a migraine. The twins were Lower School legends. Being mates with them would change my class status from fool to cool in zero seconds"

"You do mean the Simpkins twins, don't you?" I said. "Because I'm going to be really disappointed if you don't."

"Yes, of course I do," Uncle Fitz said.

"Good." I flashed him a smile. "And now, I have something to tell you. It's about the…"

Before I could say 'prowler', Hurricane Gremlin swept in and onto the table. Snatching up the milk jug, it drowned the crumpets and then bolted with the toast rack. Uncle Fitz sprang to his feet.

"I'd better make sure it doesn't choke."

I grabbed at his sleeve as he passed me. "Wait, I really need to tell you…" But I held thin air, Uncle Fitz had gone. That hairy octopus had managed it again. Knowing that it was pointless trying to distract Uncle Fitz's attention from the Gremlin, I switched thoughts to the Simpkins instead. If I could manage to be seen with the twins before school, there'd be an instant feed around 7Y that I'd made friends in high places. I'd so have street cred. I left for school feeling quite positive, unaware that the day would turn out to hold more surprises than a box of Christmas crackers.

Chapter 3

Mr Worthington – Worst Teacher Ever!

I didn't like Friday mornings. On top of the usual 'amusing' comments about the car and Victor's driving, it was also Miss Rosewater's Gate Duty day. She tackled the job pretty much like an army training officer. Miss Rosewater's nature didn't live up to her name.

"Quick! Rosie's already started!"

It was Arjun. I spun round. Wow, was he being *friendly*? No. He was talking to the village kids spilling out of the minibus. Several of the girls went egg white and immediately whipped the fluorescent scrunchies from their ponytails. Miss Rosewater had a real thing against any attempt to trendy up school uniform. She'd already herded her first victims to one side in what everybody called 'Rosie's Roundup.'

Also lurking about was Mr Worthington. No, not lurking. Hunting. His focus slithered from student to student and fixed on me. I shivered. What'd I done? I hadn't been here for more than five minutes! Mr Worthington opened his mouth to speak, but another voice, blasting out from a different direction, beat him to it.

"Kade Jones!" The voice was Miss Rosewater's. She loomed over me, tongue clicking in disapproval, her thin, angular frame all sharp points. Her other nickname was 'The Praying Mantis.' "Those are *not* regulation shoes!"

I looked down at my feet. After the milk and toast, the Gremlin had gorged itself on footwear. Racing to snatch a pair of shoes before they were all digested, I'd grabbed the nearest, not realising they were black trainers. Damn. Stupid Gremlin had done it again!

"Over there. NOW." Miss Rosewater jerked her head in the direction of her roundup as Mr Worthington bulldozed across the playground, scattering kids left, right and centre.

"Miss Rosewater. Allow me to take Kade off your hands; he and I need a chat."

Miss Rosewater swung around; her head spliced the air. Mr Worthington took a hasty step back. Any later and he'd have been knocked out.

"He's mine." Miss Rosewater was a firm believer in finders-keepers.

Mr Worthington breathed out a fake, apologetic sigh. "I'm afraid this can't wait."

Miss Rosewater pouted. She stuck her hands on her hips, invisible mandibles twitching. "He's not wearing proper uniform. That makes him *my* problem."

Mr Worthington hmphed. "Kade, you're a disgrace. Don't worry, Miss Rosewater, I'll deal with the shoes." He threw in a softener. "Less paperwork for you."

Miss Rosewater scowled but gave in. Although probably because her herd was bolting. She snaked me a *'next time'* look before galloping off.

Mr Worthington's gaze fell back on me. "My room. Now." He slammed round and marched off, carving a path through the crowd. I followed his evil footsteps to Room 101.

The way he closed the door behind us when we got there did zero to calm my nerves. Every hair on the back of my neck fizzed as Mr Worthington leant against his desk, cracking his fingers. I had a weird sense of déjà vu. If the rest of 7Y had been there, I'd have sworn that time had reversed itself to yesterday.

"Young man," Mr Worthington said, when he'd reached finger number ten. "Following yesterday's excuse that a Gremlin had digested your homework, although annoyed, I did have to admire your imagination."

As Mr Worthington was seriously lacking in the admiration department for anyone in school uniform, this was hard to believe. I started a slow backwards shuffle towards the door, calculating how many steps I needed to take before I could escape.

"Stop fidgeting!" The real Mr Worthington leapt out. Sucking in a deep breath, he wrestled it back in. I bumped my schoolbag down my arm. If necessary, I could slug him with it. Putting on a creepy smile, Mr Worthington offered me a sweet from a packet on his desk. "Have a mint. Oh, and could I have your phone?"

The tone was all nicety-nice. This doubled the creepiness. He was like the Big Bad Wolf from the Red Riding Hood story, and in the original version things hadn't ended well. Why did he want my phone? I wished I could read his mind.

Mr Worthington shook his head. "I know you have it. You kids are never without your mobiles; it's like going out with no clothes." He stuck out a hand. "Give." We observed each other in cold silence. "I said give." There was clear threat in his voice.

My heart rattled against my ribcage like a fraught budgie trying to escape. "I... I can't" My words stuttered out. I don't have it. The Gremlin flushed it down the loo. Honest, it did," I added as a whole series of emotions, none of them pleasant, flickered across Mr Worthington's face. I held my breath so long and hard that my ears buzzed. When he eventually spoke, I leapt higher than a freaked-out kangaroo.

"Breathe, before you pass out." Mr Worthington sucked in his thin lips so far that he almost swallowed them. "After our exchange yesterday, I happened to see something. In your phone's photo collection. A picture of a very strange, but undoubtedly very real, creature."

What? My phone had been locked. How had he been able to go nosing around looking at my photos? Who did he think he was? Head of MI5? Black Ops?

"You hacked me?" I almost choked in outrage. "You're not allowed to do that!"

Mr Worthington didn't appear to be bothered. Wait until I got Uncle Fitz to make a complaint, he'd be bothered then... hang on, what picture of a very strange creature?

Mr Worthington slid a hand into his jacket pocket

and plucked out a photo. He shoved it under my nose. "I made multiple prints."

I practically fainted. There, in front of me in full fanged glory was the Gremlin, tentacles arranged like a hairy Hawaiian skirt. That explained the thing's obsession with my phone. It was into selfies!

"For once you were telling the truth." Mr Worthington crossed his arms. "But I'll bet it's more than that hairy fairy your uncle has scuttling about. I reckon there's a whole creature collection. Must be very valuable. And dangerous." He stared over my head. "And illegal."

Opening his briefcase, Mr Worthington produced two more photos and a pair of leather monogrammed gloves, which he tossed aside. He slapped the photos on the table. One showed Glenda collecting the washing. The other Me, Myself and I. As he was running off, the biggest thing in shot apart from the trees, was his tushi, but his heads were unmistakable.

I felt sick. My gaze travelled to meet Mr Worthington's. He stood there, tall, lanky and mean. Something inside my brain clicked. In my head, I time-travelled back to yesterday evening: standing by the garden wall being nuked under the prowler's burning glare. A shiver ran through me. Mr Worthington reminded me of... of... I ogled the photos again. Then...

"You're the prowler!" I yelped. "It's you who's been stalking Grosse Manor!"

Mr Worthington raised amused eyebrows. "Maybe," he said, examining his nails.

Despite being scared, I was angry too. I balled my fists. "You can be arrested for that. Trespassing's illegal. It's BAD."

Mr Worthington considered this. "True. But not as bad as your father leaving you with someone whose idea of a cuddly pet is the stuff of nightmares." He tapped the Gremlin's photo. "Nothing could save you from this thing's fangs. Not even a rabies shot. Your uncle should be locked up."

This wound me up even more. I can insult Uncle Fitz, we're related, but nobody else had the right. "Actually," I said, voice tight, "my uncle's a highly respected zoologist."

"Shove the blood's thicker than water rubbish." Mr Worthington let free a nasty laugh. "What other creatures does your uncle have?" He snapped his fingers under my nose. "Come on. Or perhaps you'd rather tell Social Services?"

Absolutely not. The last thing I wanted was Social Services at the door; along with a squadron of S.A.S soldiers; an overseas warrant for Dad's arrest; and a strait jacket for Uncle Fitz. As for me? I preferred not to think about that.

"Don't worry," Mr Worthington said in response to my silence. "I already know."

Darn, he really had been stalking the Manor. Luckily, the registration bell rang. Mr Worthington vacuumed in his lips, livid that time had saved me. For now.

"Another thing." Mr Worthington's hand shot out. Grabbing my tie, he reeled me in. I could smell coffee on his breath. "I'm very interested in your uncle and his pets, so here's the deal. You'll be my daily diary of life at Grosse Manor and I'll not talk to Social Services." His tone held an unpleasant, seedy silkiness. "And keep quiet about our little talk, or," A long, ominous pause. "Believe me when I say you'll find out." He released me with a push. "Get it?"

"Yeah," I muttered. "I get it."

"Then get out. And remember, I have powerful

friends. And your contact details." Mr Worthington was worse than the Gremlin.

During form time, instead of solving the daily word puzzle, I focused instead on the bigger challenge set by Mr Worthington. Luckily, next week was half-term, which gave me nine days to come up with a plan. Today, I'd have to cope. I didn't have Maths until this afternoon, so I was safe until then. At break and lunch time I'd hide in the boys' toilets.

The second the bell rang for break, I legged it for the bogs. I'd have made it too if the Simpkins twins hadn't grabbed me. One of them, Joss, stuck out an arm. I knew it was him by the black ear stud. The stud broke school rules, but the twins were so ultra-identical that the teachers let it go. It was how they told them apart.

"Hey, Kade," Joss said, loud enough for Arjun to hear. "We still on for after school?"

"Yeah, we've been trying to get inside your house for years," Calvin added, flicking back a curtain of dark hair. I nodded, stuck between not wanting to bump into Mr Worthington, and pride that the heroes of Lower School were talking to me.

"See you later," Calvin said.

"See you," Joss echoed. "Oh, and Arj, look after our mate here, okay?"

The twins sauntered off, leaving Arjun along with his cronies; Paul Davies and Jakub Mazur shuffling their feet and nudging each other. Eventually, Arjun acted as spokesperson. He held out a bag of toffees. "Want a sweet?"

And that was that. Next lesson, Arjun shoved Tom Riley's bag off the chair so he could sit next to me, and at lunchtime insisted that I joined him, Paul and Jacob outside. Although it was much better than having lunch on my own, I found their U-turn a bit suspicious. On the other hand, it was a chance to find out more about the village.

"In Grosse, we're all from unique backgrounds," Jacob said, offering me a crisp. "Ask Paul. He's descended from a long line of Doppelgangers."

"Not evil ones," Paul put in quickly, seeing my expression. "Although I'd like their abilities. Think how cool it'd be if you could transform yourself into a mind-reading, mind-wiping clone. My Great Uncle Albert has the talent," he continued. "If you can call it that if you do it in reverse. Not good. Once, he accidentally got Mum reading his mind about her cooking. Believe me, the ending to that wasn't pretty."

They also talked about why the villagers' preferred to go unnoticed.

"Nobody wants to be a tourist attraction," said Jacob.

"Or be made to take part in scientific experiments," put in Arjun.

"Or be burnt at the stake," added Paul. "That's also in my family history."

Same as me, the village kids had to keep non-village friendships off- premises, although this had perks. On his last birthday, Jakub's parents had taken the whole class to a theme park even though it had been mega expensive. Partly because someone had thrown up in the minibus and Jakub's dad had had to pay for the cleaning. They also told me why I'd been ignored.

"You weren't exactly friendly," Paul said. "We kept angling for invites to come and see the Gremlin; but you kept making excuses. In the end we decided you were a snob."

"Uncle Fitz says no visitors," I answered.

"But not us. He must have told you that we weren't a

problem," Jakub objected. I could tell that he didn't believe me.

I gave a hollow laugh. "He's not one for details. Protecting his critters comes first, last, and everything in-between. Why else would I keep to myself?"

Jakub shrugged. "How'd I know?"

I slammed my sandwich box shut. "You could've asked. You all knew about the Manor; I didn't have a clue about you!"

Jakub retaliated. The next second we were both up on our feet in a stand-off. "You're saying your attitude problem's *our* fault?"

Arjun noticed the Simpkins observing from a distance. He grabbed me by the elbow and tugged me back down onto the bench. "It's cool, guys!" he called, sending a breezy wave in their direction. Then to Jakub, "Shut it. I want those football cards."

"What?" It was as if someone had thrown a bucket of cold water over me. I'd *known* there was something funny going on. I jerked my arm free. "You're being paid to be nice?"

The three of them went all edgy. Paul developed a huge obsession with a passing fly.

"Course not," Arjun said, quickly, whilst at the same time Jakub came out with a yes.

I rounded on Paul. "And what do you have to say?"

"That I'd prefer to keep out of it." Paul buried himself in his packet of crisps.

Arjun intervened. "Fine then. Joss and Calvin did say they'd give us their England Team football cards if we'd make friends with you, but be honest, Kade, you *did* come over all stuck-up even if you didn't mean to. We'll cancel that thought now, okay?"

"I do want to see the Gremlin, though," Paul put in.

"Believe me," I said. "You don't."

"If it helps," Arjun said, "we've always thought you're brave. We're too scared to wind Mr Worthington up. Though telling him that the Gremlin had eaten your homework was risky. That's why I was so mad at you," he added. "But your nerve was awesome."

Ha! If that was true, then they were way off mark. Anyway, at that moment Paul spotted a cricket ball lurking in the drain and attempted to defuse the situation by picking up the ball and lobbing it at me.

"Catch!" he called. My arm reacted ahead of my brain (that's what seven years of cricket practice does for you). In other words before I could tell Paul to get lost.

"Brilliant!" The P.E teacher who'd been crossing the yard rushed up. "Really excellent reflexes. I expect to see you at the next cricket practice. Come on, let's see what else you've got. You." She pointed at Arjun, Paul and Jacob. "Be his feeders."

This led to a bit of impromptu showing off on my part. The clapping from a watching crowd of other kids did a lot to improve my mood. When someone called out to the teacher that I was good with a football too, I started re-evaluating Grosse High. This mood swing also spilt over into how I should deal with Mr Worthington's threat. I so wasn't going to be blackmailed into spying on Uncle Fitz. His idea of what made a good family pet might be weird, but he wasn't doing anything wrong. And he trusted me.

I put a hard spin on the ball as I threw it to Arjun. I needed a plan to out-manoeuvre Mr Worthington. Something he wouldn't realise until too late. Something out-of-the-box (in other words devious). I was good at that. Quite often I did it without noticing. My sub-conscious worked away at the problem all on its own until it found a solution and then handed it over, gift-wrapped.

"Oy!" Arjun protested, dropping the spinning ball. "That hurt."

A sneaky grin snuck across my lips. Not because of Arjun's stinging hands but because I now knew exactly how to deal with my Maths teacher. Until I sussed his game, I'd let him think he had me trapped. Anything he wanted to know I'd invent. That couldn't harm Uncle Fitz. Why was he nosing after him? Or was it the Monsters? Did he think that disclosing their existence would make him famous? Or was he planning on carrying out a little blackmail? Once I knew, I'd tell Uncle Fitz and suggest that we found a Doppelganger who, unlike Paul's Uncle Albert, could do their job properly and wipe Mr Worthington's mind. Problem solved. I'd be a hero, Uncle Fitz'd be happy, and Dad would have to apologise for calling me selfish and irresponsible. Maybe he'd change his mind about staying at Grosse Manor too and we'd move back to London. Or at least let me visit Arnie.

After that, the day's upward trend continued because Mr Worthington twisted his ankle and had to go home. We had a supply teacher for Maths who didn't give us any homework and let us pack up early. This meant I made it to the school gates double quick to wait for Joss and Calvin. Victor pipped the car horn.

I glared at him through the driver's window. "Do you have to do that?"

Looking very glum, Victor pointed an accusing finger at the girl sitting next to him.

"Miss Awful Simpkins," he announced in a flat tone.

I'd forgotten about the twins' sister.

"Ivy, *not* Awful," the girl corrected, swinging round. Her thick, dark brown, tightly braided hair followed her in a swift swish. "Victor picked me up from school, but he's not very happy about it."

"Miss Awful has problems with my driving," Victor said, his voice tighter than the skin stretched over his high cheekbones. "Despite having driven cars for more than sixty years."

"Perhaps that's the problem," Ivy retorted. "Maybe it'd be a good idea to stop."

Victor's hands tightened on the wheel. He started the engine with unusual force.

"Mind the Crossing Officer," Ivy told him. "You nearly ran her over before."

"I didn't see her." Victor growled from deep in his throat.

"How?" Ivy asked. "Her stick's as big as a giant's lollypop and she's not much smaller. Anyway, we can't go, we have to wait for my brothers." She tapped her watch. "They need to improve their timekeeping."

Ivy was a girl of very big opinions, the total opposite of her size and appearance: small, skinny and unremarkable except for her large eyes and long lashes, both as dark and velvety as treacle. They reminded me of a baby seal.

Ivy caught me staring. She preened. "I'm descended from a long line of Cornish Selkies on Mum's side of the family. It's why I'm so good at swimming." She was good at criticising too. Having finished with Victor and her brothers, she started on me. "You're a bit scruffy. You've lost the top button from your shirt and your tie has a stain on it. What did you spill?"

I flushed. "Mind your own business. Even better, mind Victor's." The missing button was Mr Worthington's fault.

Ivy smiled, not at all put out. "I will. He could do with the help."

Victor's fingers twitched. Fortunately, (or not, depending on how you want to look at it) the twins' arrival averted bloodshed.

"Hey, guys," said Joss as he wrenched the car door open and slid in followed by Calvin.

"Why are you sitting up front, Ivy? It's Kade's car not yours."

"Victor needs help with his driving technique," Ivy answered.

I'm not sure if the growling came from the engine or Victor as he hit the accelerator. I grinned. If Ivy kept going (she did) we'd be home in half the usual time. Her constant criticisms thinly disguised as 'helpful comments' transformed Victor into a racing driver. He slammed on the brakes in the nick of time to avoid taking out the manor gates. Everyone surged forwards, held back from saying goodbye to life solely because the car had really good seatbelts. Victor folded his arms.

"One of you needs to get out, open the gates and then close them again."

"Why?" I said, re-swallowing lunch. "Uncle Fitz always keeps them locked."

"Not today," Victor said. "The Gremlin's hidden the fobs. Sir Fitz tried a padlock, but of course the nuisance went and swallowed the key." He made this sound as if it was our fault.

"Come on; somebody hop out and open the gates. I need to be off as soon as I can. The wife wants to go shopping."

Although I totally believed him about the Gremlin, I was less convinced about the needing to be off bit. It wasn't like Victor to miss an opportunity for the Car Door

43

Game. It turned out that today he was replacing it with the fun pastime of 'Get Your Own Back'.

The second we got to the house Victor actioned his cunning plan. Unfolding his lanky frame, he creaked out of the car, crunched across the gravel and flung open the front passenger door.

"Madam," he said, with a politeness that wouldn't have fooled the thickest of braindead zombies.

Ivy stopped picking her nails and got out. I winced as the gargantuan form of Me, Myself and I galloped down the stone steps, woofing and slobbering, intent on reaching the small figure directly in his path. Delighted at the prospect of making a new friend, the dog headed straight for her. I took a sharp breath, but Ivy was unfazed.

"Sit!" she commanded, one small finger pointing.

To my amazement, the twins' un-amazement and Victor's disappointment, Me, Myself and I skidded to a halt, bottom fixed firmly on the ground.

"Good boy." Ivy's small hand patted each head. "It's all in the voice," she explained. "You have to be firm." She pranced off up the stone steps and into the house leaving Victor glaring at the dog. The dog didn't care; he'd found a biscuit.

"Kade!" Nano seconds later, Ivy was back, bouncing up and down on the top step and waving her arms about like a castaway on a desert island who'd seen a rescue boat. "Kade! Come inside! Your housekeeper says your uncle's having a nervous breakdown in his study!"

"It'll be that stupid Gremlin again," I told the twins. "It always is."

But once I'd climbed the steps with the twins behind me and even before we entered the house, it was clear something was massively wrong. The place was too quiet.

At the very least, there should have been the sounds of the Gremlin's latest attempts at mass destruction. Major warning alarms started clanging furiously inside my head. Dropping my schoolbag, I shot off down the long, narrow hallway to Uncle Fitz's study. Everyone (including the dog) followed. Outside the room, one hand on the battered oak door, I paused. Did the situation call for immediate entry, or should I knock? Calvin solved the problem by walking into me.

"Whoops, sorry," he apologised as my head whammed the door open.

But Uncle Fitz, slumped pale and comatose in his leather armchair, was oblivious. Glenda, fanning him with a large book, sent me urgent signals.

"It's the Gremlin," she moaned. "*It's gone!*"

Chapter 4

One of our Monsters is Missing

It was true. The Gremlin had vanished. Leaving a real mess too. Glass from the shattered window spiked the floor. The fancy (though strongly re-enforced) iron grille attached over the pane from outside lay at an angle in the Gremlin's blanketed nest. Blimey, how strong was the mutant monkey? Even King Kong would've struggled with shifting that grille!

"Was the grille properly screwed in, Uncle Fitz?" I asked.

"Absolutely!" Uncle Fitz looked a bit miffed at being asked. "I did it myself."

"Any possibility the Gremlin used an electric drill?"

"No," Uncle Fitz said, even more indignant. "It wouldn't do that." Me, Myself and I rummaged through the Gremlin's nest with his nose and dragged out a chew toy. A metal drill attachment rolled out with it. Uncle Fitz blushed. "Well, maybe."

Apparently, the Gremlin had been going nuts all day, tearing around like a hyper-active baboon. Uncle Fitz had finally been forced into action after it had leapt onto his shoulders during lunch and shoved his head into the soup.

"I thought it was over-tired, so I put it down for a nap," he said.

Glenda gave him a pointed look. Uncle Fitz flushed. "I did have to chase it around the house first with a butterfly net," he admitted.

"So, when did you discover it was missing?" I asked.

"About three hours ago. I found all this mess and the Gremlin gone. At first, I thought it'd snuck off into the grounds and would come back, but it hasn't. Glenda and I have searched the whole estate." Uncle Fitz's eyebrows and moustache twitched at supersonic speed. "What if it's hurt? Or... or" Uncle Fitz started shaking, "...been *kidnapped?*"

"There's glass outside too," I said, leaning out of the small window. "And a couple of big bolts. Maybe someone did break in instead of the Gremlin breaking out. But who'd take it?"

"Who'd want it?" Glenda muttered.

"It must be the prowler," Uncle Fitz said, twisting his hands in despair.

"What prowler?" Ivy's ears pricked up. Things were becoming more interesting for the Simpkins by the second.

"We have a prowler," I said. "I've seen them."

"*Seen them?*" Uncle Fitz staggered backwards in shock. "When? Why didn't you tell me?"

"I tried to. Three times."

"Then you should have tried harder!" Uncle Fitz gripped his hair with both hands.

"Don't blame me," I said, nettled. "I did my best. It's not my fault that you kept running off." I kept back the information that I knew who the prowler was because I didn't have proof. It'd be my word against Mr Worthington's and grown-ups tend to believe other grown-ups. "Have you called the police?" I asked instead. "They can come and test for fingerprints."

Uncle Fitz immediately started searching the walls for invisible prints. "I've called our local constabulary. Eric's sent Joe out on a search for the Gremlin."

"Eric Huddle's our Chief Constable," Joss explained. "And Joe's his nephew. They're our Grosse Village Police Force."

Uncle Fitz ran a trembling hand through his hair. I decided this wasn't the best time to tell him that Mr Worthington was his prowler. He was already stressed out. I'd wait until this Chief Constable Huddle arrived, get his take on things, and then break the news. In the meantime, Uncle Fitz needed something to focus on.

"Uncle Fitz, why don't you search the grounds again? Maybe the Gremlin's playing hide and seek." I nodded in the direction of the Simpkins. "We'll search the house."

The ploy worked. A spark of renewed hope rebooted

Uncle Fitz. "Good thinking. The Simpkins can help with your jobs. Oh, and keep the dog inside. I don't want him going missing too." He hurried out, Glenda following.

Joss nudged me. "About this prowler; what's going on? You saw someone?"

"Yeah," I said. "Yesterday whilst I was walking the dog. They fell out of a tree right next to me and then legged it."

Ivy winced. "Painful. Can you describe them?"

"No. They were wearing one of those steam-punk balaclavas. They were tall though. And thin."

"A masked intruder," Joss said. "Anything else strange been happening?"

I thought about the letter that Uncle Fitz had whisked under the table at breakfast. Was it connected to the Gremlin's disappearance? I didn't see the harm in sharing the information.

"Uncle Fitz was a bit odd at breakfast. Well, he's usually odd, but I mean odder than normal. He had a letter that he didn't want me to see. He hid it."

The Simpkins lit up with curiosity.

"Who do you think it was from?" Joss asked.

"Maybe the prowler," I said. "Perhaps they're trying to blackmail Uncle Fitz. It's a bit of a coincidence that he gets a letter that he won't talk about, then BAM! The Gremlin's vanished."

"So, you think they nicked it?" Calvin said.

"See all that?" I pointed at the glass scattered over the room. There'd be less if the window had been smashed from the inside. Then there's the grille. If the Gremlin ripped it off the wall, why not simply drop it? Especially as it was fixed to the outside. It's more like somebody wanted to get *in*. Either to nick the Gremlin or let it escape. That'd explain the glass on the path. It'd have knocked out the bits when it climbed through."

Calvin and Joss were impressed.

"Good thinking, Sherlock," Calvin said.

I waved a modest hand.

"It's my thing.

"Don't get too pleased with yourself," Ivy said. "Because you've totally forgotten to back up your theory with evidence of outside help. Like footprints. We should go and search."

"And disturb the crime scene?" I tutted. "And that goes for in here too, so don't touch!"

Ivy's fingers were probing the Gremlin's nest.

"See?" Calvin wagged a finger at his sister. "Kade's on it. Get your hands off."

"We need to wait for your Chief Constable," I said. "Is he good?"

The Simpkins exchanged looks.

"Umm, depends on what you mean by good," Joss replied. "To be fair to Huddle, there's not a lot of crime in Grosse Village so he doesn't get much practice. Oy!"

Something round and red hit Joss's nose. It was an apple followed by a raucous laugh.

"Ooh, a pack of kiddies. Time for yum yums!"

Perched parrot-style on the window ledge squatted a short, stocky being with more hair than any person should have. It was one of Uncle Fitz's Trolls. "Bit of a mess, innit? Lotta cleanin' ter do. Now, who could be responsible, ay?"

"You?" I said. The Trolls liked to indulge in a bit of vandalism if the opportunity arose.

"Maybe," said the Troll, exploring his nostrils with a dirty finger.

"If it was you, where's the Gremlin?" Ivy asked.

"Don't know wot yer mean," the Troll said. "Or *do* I?" He waggled his ears, enjoying himself. "You," the Troll pointed at Calvin, "would look very appertisin' roastin' on a spit with an apple in yer gob."

"And you'd look good by leaving," I shot back. Then to the Simpkins, "Ignore him. Uncle Fitz doesn't let the Trolls eat people."

The Troll glared. He wriggled around and twerked his rear end at us before scrabbling out of the broken window. We heard him scuttling down the wall.

"Cool," said Joss. "I can't wait to see the rest of the Monsters in-between searching for the Gremlin. Exploring this place is like playing Halloween Hide n' Seek; you never know what's going to jump out at you."

Deciding that the best way to search was from the bottom up, we started in the cellar. Unfortunately, as with the Gremlin's nest, Ivy insisted on looking with her hands. She poked the Dragon's nose. As Old Smokey doesn't particularly enjoy having a finger jabbed up his left nostril, this wasn't much appreciated. With a deep, rumbling belly growl, he pushed back his spiny ears and belched out a long stream of angry red fire at Ivy, who hopped out of the way.

"Hmm," she said as the whitewashed wall frazzled to smoky black.

Joss wagged a disapproving finger at her. "Behave. You almost got fried."

Ivy ignored him. She snatched the duty list from me.

"What's next? Oh, the Trolls."

"They live in a bathroom over in the East Wing. Well, the toilet," I said. "It's been specially enlarged. On the way up, if everyone checks a different room for the Gremlin, we can cover four at a time."

But none of the rooms contained a hidden Gremlin.

Ivy got excited thinking that she'd heard it as we climbed the East Wing's staircase, but it was the Trolls. When we walked into their bathroom, they were busy tying each other up with loo roll. (Their second favourite game next to flushing each other down the u-bend, which explained their unique aroma.)

"What a waste," said Ivy in a loud, disapproving voice. A Troll lobbed a loo roll at her. Ivy retaliated by smacking him on the head with it. The Troll yelped and called her a rude name. Ivy duffed him again, plus two of his mates who got in the way. This was enough to inform the Trolls that things were not quite as they should be in the Land of Bathroom. They fell quiet, looking from their clobbered companions, to Ivy, to the toilet roll, and back again. Simmering silence gave way to low mutters. Ivy stayed unbothered, which annoyed them even more.

Muttering, the Trolls gathered together in a sullen cluster like a clump of overgrown mushrooms and held a quick meeting during which Ivy received many threatening glares. Ivy yawned. This annoyed the Trolls even more. With a last mutter, they dispersed. Ivy found herself enclosed in a moving circle as the Trolls chanted...

"'Orrid little Missy, serve 'er on a dishy,

Cut 'er into pieces and play with the bones!"

A Troll reached out and gave Ivy a sharp pinch with his bony fingers.

"Oy!" I said. "Leave her alone. You started it, not her." But the pinch didn't have the desired effect anyhow.

Ivy laughed. "Really? Is that all you have? A stupid rhyme and some skipping in a circle? That is *so* pathetic. Frankly, I expected more."

Pinching Troll leant towards Ivy again, index finger and thumb clicking open and shut like a crab's claw.

Grabbing a loofah from the bath shelf, I brandished it in the air.

"Hey! I said, enough!"

The Troll looked at the loofah and burst into loud, derisive laughter.

"Yer need to do better than that! That's nowt more than a dead sea sponge," he cackled.

To prove his point, he extended a veiny arm towards me. Wrong. A loofah, used correctly, is so much more than a back scrubber. It makes a fantastic cricket bat. Before he could dodge: **SMACK!** I sent the Troll sailing across the bathroom, straight into the open loo. The Trolls roared in fury.

"Careful, Kade!" Calvin yelled.

"Yeah, re-enforcements closing in from behind!" Joss clarified the warning. I swung round in time to see three more Trolls advancing from behind. The rest of the tribe moved in on the twins for grassing them up. But they'd made a serious tactical error; they'd forgotten about Ivy.

"Don't worry, guys, I'll use my self-defence skills!" Ivy called, smacking one of my would-be attackers on the head with a towel and kickboxing his two mates who flew high up in the air. They thudded down like concrete rain.

Unprepared and unused to counterattack, the Trolls froze, their mouths clanging open in shock (Trolls' jaws unhinge like a snake's) revealing a jumble of brown, broken teeth. Then, deciding that their best remaining option was to withdraw, they ran. In front of, behind and over each other, screaming and waving skinny arms in their scramble for the safety of the toilet. The last Troll in slammed the lid shut. I knelt on it whilst Ivy flushed the chain repetitively until the howling Monsters, unable to get down the u-bend due to overcrowding, begged for mercy.

"There you go," Ivy said with a grin, as we high-fived. "How to deal with Trolls. Let's do the same with your prowler."

"Talking of which," Joss said to his siblings, "don't tell Mum and Dad or they might put the kybosh on us coming over."

"Good idea," Calvin agreed. "They don't have a problem with prowling Monsters but I'm not sure about human ones."

"I think I speak for the three of us," said Joss, "that as descendants of strange but true ancestry ourselves, we have a duty to help Kade solve the mystery of the Problem Prowler. Wonder what they're after?"

"Profit?" Calvin suggested. "Maybe the prowler knows about the Monsters and wants to sell them. Imagine how much dosh you'd make if you sold a Monster."

Unknowingly, Calvin had echoed my own thoughts. I hoped he couldn't tell. I liked the Simpkins, but I was waiting for the Chief Constable before coming clean about everything.

"Sir Fitz says stop yacking; the Yeti's getting in a flap!" Glenda's disembodied voice wailed up through the floorboards.

"Amelia's always in a flap," I said. "Usually about the temperature of her room. We'd better go and see what's wrong."

But Amelia had to wait because Chief Constable Huddle arrived.

Huddle's approach to detective work wasn't cutting edge. He stood in the middle of the Gremlin's room, clueless.

"And you think the Gremlin either escaped or someone kidnapped it?" he finally said. "Now, what makes you say that?"

"Oh, I don't know," I replied. "The wrenched-out grille? The drill attachment? The broken glass?"

"Which would you say is more likely?" Huddle scribbled away in his notebook.

"There's more glass inside than out, which suggests a break-in." I spoke again for Uncle Fitz who didn't seem up to answering questions. "Although earlier on a Troll did hint that they might be responsible."

Huddle scribbled away some more. Ivy peered at his writing.

"You've spelt responsible wrong. It's ible not able."

Huddle flushed and stuck the notebook back in his pocket.

"Anything else, Fitz?" he asked, turning his back on Ivy. Uncle Fitz shook his head.

"Uncle Fitz, the *letter*." I said. "The one you were reading at breakfast and hid."

Uncle Fitz flushed. "That was nothing, Kade," he mumbled, in a way that completely said the opposite. "I told you. Junk mail. I let the Gremlin have it." He pointed to a mangled strip of paper in the Gremlin's nest. "There it is."

I picked up the mashed bit of pulp. If I applied a tonne of imagination, I could probably hazard a guess that it was part of a letter. Or not. To be honest it was impossible to tell.

Huddle adjusted his Police Officer's cap. "I think I've seen everything."

"But you haven't examined the crime scene from outside!" I shook my head, stupefied. Huddle was less use than a chocolate teapot. No way was I telling him

55

about Mr Worthington. Huddle flushed again, muttering under his breath that kids of today were know-alls.

So let's go outside then," he snapped, stomping out.

Joss muttered in my ear as we followed. "Do you believe your uncle?"

"No," I murmured back. "But short of rifling through his mail there's nothing I can do."

Outside, more evidence pointed to the Trolls. Imprints of clawed feet criss-crossed the gravel plotting a path to the long, jagged, fingernail scratches on the wall. These led to the smashed window. A tree, growing alongside the house wall, looked like it had been attacked by several tornadoes and then another for good measure. Broken branches peeled away at agonised angles, drooping like fractured limbs.

"Those are definitely from the Trolls," Uncle Fitz said, pointing to the scratches.

"Then I know who the culprits are." Huddle hauled out his notebook again and scribbled in it. "It's the Trolls who set the Gremlin free, Fitz. I expect it'll come back when it's hungry." He put the notebook away.

Unbelievable. "Is that it?" I said.

Huddle swallowed an impatient humph. I could tell I was getting on his nerves. "You're a very... persistent young man, aren't you?"

"Not half as persistent as the Press will be if someone reports seeing the Gremlin leaping across the moors." I said.

"Everybody in the village knows what the Gremlin looks like – and to keep their mouths shut." Huddle batted back.

"Grosse Village is hardly the whole of Cornwall." Calvin took my side.

56

"I hadn't thought of that." Huddle gave a worried blink.

"I suppose it might get mistaken for a mutant monkey," Joss mused. "You know, escaped from a research laboratory?"

"Good thinking, Calvin." Huddle cheered up.

"I'm Joss." Joss tapped his earring.

"You should know that," Ivy told Huddle. "You brought him home after he fainted in your wife's salon when he had it pierced."

Both Joss and Huddle targeted Ivy with murderous scowls.

"Perhaps you could search the moors again, Chief Constable?" I suggested.

"Good idea." Ivy, the verbal assassin, gave a fake sigh. "Shame our brother, Ben, isn't here with one of his surveillance gadgets. *He'd* find the Gremlin in seconds. But then, he's *naturally good* at investigative work."

I thought Huddle was going to explode. He stomped back to his car, ignoring my suggestion of a full area check, so as to positively confirm that the Trolls were guilty. I made a mental note to do it myself. At that moment, from way above, a series of painful, though strangely tuneful cries, slammed into our ears. High up, a window cracked.

"The Gremlin's back!" said Joss. "Problem solved."

"No," I said, as more soulful yelps tumbled down. A slate slid off the roof. "It's the Yeti. We'd better go up. We can carry on checking rooms on the way."

Amelia had a room on the third floor, converted by Uncle Fitz into a sauna. Unlike other Yetis, whose thick fur keeps them warm in the world's coldest snows, Amelia required Equatorial temperatures. Uncle Fitz had discovered her huddled up at the back of a Himalayan cave, suffering from hypothermia. After thawing her out through the combined use of a dozen sleeping bags, six thermal blankets, and a fire of volcanic heat, he'd brought her to Grosse Manor with the promise that she wouldn't ever be cold again.

"Never mind," Ivy said, stroking the Yeti's silky, white fur. "I'll knit you a warm scarf for Christmas. I'll make it so long that you'll be able to wrap it three times around your neck."

Amelia smiled adoringly at Ivy who patted her massive paw and emptied more water over the hot coals, discharging a cloud of thick, scalding steam. I felt my eyeballs dehydrate.

"Let's go before we get heatstroke," I said.

We left Amelia basking in steam and headed downstairs. Halfway, we met Uncle Fitz, struggling under the weight of an old family portrait from the hallway. At least it was a painting until it morphed into me wearing Ivy's plaits and school dress.

"Shape-Shifter," Uncle Fitz panted. "From Eric. He's asked me to try and sort it out. It's his cousin's pet. She brought it back from Italy, but it's got issues. Shapeshifters lack their own form, so they mimic. This one's hyperactive and keeps shifting shape every few seconds."

On cue, the Shapeshifter shifted into a shoe, a statue and then a piece of stair carpet with Uncle Fitz's false foot sticking out before keeling over with a sad whimper.

"It needs to rest in an empty room." Uncle Fitz rolled the Shapeshifter up. "Perhaps you could all lend a hand getting it to the attic?"

"You guys go ahead," I said. "I need to bring my schoolbag in from the step." This was true, but it also gave me the chance to search outside whilst everybody else was occupied.

Unfortunately, I didn't do any better than Huddle. The house was too tall. I needed a ladder to root out any possible evidence that might be higher up, trapped in the tree. Stepping back to get a better view, I leant against a bush. Scrunching myself further against it, my foot pressed down on something soft and hidden from sight. Worried that I'd squashed some poor little animal, I lifted my foot. My gaze dropped down onto a small, black lump squatting on the soil. Giving it a careful poke with my toe, the thing unfurled. I yelped, worried it was about to bite. False alarm. Now that it lay flat, it was obvious that it wasn't an animal at all. It was a black leather glove with two initials neatly monogrammed in gold: **C.W**.

CW? Stooping, I picked up the glove. The long fingers dangled over the side of my hand like gargantuan tarantula legs. Whose was it? Not Uncle Fitz's: it was too big, and the first initial was wrong. But there was something about it that was familiar. The next second, I let out a terrified squeal, dropping the glove as if it really was a deadly spider. I knew who it belonged to. I'd seen it in the Maths room in a certain teacher's briefcase. The C.W stood for C Worthington.

But how could Mr Worthington have even got here, let alone climb up the tree when he'd twisted his ankle in front of everyone in the staffroom?

Unless he'd been faking.

Chapter 5

Where oh where has the Gremlin Gone?

Totally freaked out by what the glove meant, my first thought was to tell Uncle Fitz. But I very quickly changed my mind. Uncle Fitz would go straight to Huddle – Chief Constable Useless. Things wouldn't end in a good way, and psycho Worthington would wreak his revenge. I had visions of the Monsters being carted off to a top-secret research lab and Uncle Fitz to a padded cell. I sat down cross-legged on the floor to think.

A Troll strolled by. "Oh, it's you," he said, stopping next to me. "Wotcha up to?"

"Nothing," I said, shifting position so he wouldn't see the glove and ask questions. I focused on the wall, hoping he'd get the message and go away. He didn't.

"Them scratch marks is mine. I use the wall ter file me nails." The Troll showed off his long, thorny fingers. He paused, taking in the torn tree. "Who did that?"

"You tell me," I said.

The Troll huffed. "Don't be snotty. Wasn't us Trolls, we're tree fans. They're great fer hiding in."

"Maybe it was the Gremlin then," I said. "I expect you've heard it's disappeared?"

The Troll plucked a maggoty leaf from a bush and ate it. "Yep, we knows old nutjob's vamoosed. But I'm sayin' nowt." Tapping the side of his rubbery nose he skipped off with a smug grin. Still, at least I knew how the wall had been damaged.

Focusing again on the tree, I studied the pattern of its broken limbs. If Mr Worthington had climbed it to reach the window the glove might have slipped out of his pocket, landing under the bush. Or perhaps he'd fallen and that's how the glove got lost. But more important, why'd he been here? What had he been after? I remembered his fierce demands to know exactly how many Monsters Uncle Fitz had. The hairs on my neck prickled. Had Mr Worthington's plan been to steal the Gremlin all along? In my imagination, I watched him weaving his way up the tree like a giant centipede, long skinny limbs clinging to the trunk; his break-in kit stashed in a backpack (that'd explain the grille's removal), and a portable pet carrier. No doubt he'd been met with fierce resistance. If the Gremlin was happy to drown its number one fan in a bowl of soup, it wouldn't spare Mr Worthington. He'd have had a real job tackling the evil furball. In fact, it wouldn't surprise me if the thing had won and given him the slip.

Back inside the house, the Simpkins had invited themselves for a sleepover.

"It'll be like those overnighters you can do at the Natural History Museum, except with living exhibits. So cool!" Joss said excitedly.

"You won't think that when Me, Myself and I sticks his noses in your ear at stupid o'clock," I said, turning to Uncle Fitz as he came into the room. "Uncle Fitz, I met a Troll in the garden. I think he knew more than he'd say about the Gremlin's disappearance."

Uncle Fitz rocketed off to the East Wing, returning later with the information that the Gremlin had last been seen bounding off in the direction of the main gates. One of the Trolls had said that the Gremlin was chasing somebody, but another had disagreed. This had led to a big argument. Uncle Fitz had no idea who was correct as the conversation had ended with the two Trolls having a massive fight and the rest taking bets on who'd win.

"What could have happened to the darling dear?" Glenda wept, dumping soup bowls on the dining table. Good job it was soup; she was crying so hard anything solid would've disintegrated.

"Honestly, Glenda!" I wiped away tear stains from my glass. They left faint, green streaks. "You don't even like the Gremlin. Yesterday you called it a h..." Glenda cut me off with a screeching wail. The dishes rattled. I grabbed a plate before it bounced off the table.

"Do you have to do that?" I complained. "It's like sitting on the runway at Heathrow."

"I'm a Banshee," Glenda snapped. "I wail at any misfortune, remember? Liking doesn't come into it." She wailed again. This time in Ivy's ear.

Ivy winced. "Ow! You know what, Kade? I agree with you. Her voice *is* awful."

Glenda took the huff. She smacked the breadbasket down by Ivy's bowl. The soup leapt up and splattered over her school dress. Glenda smirked

"I keep wondering where my tentacled friend could be." Uncle Fitz dabbed at his eyes with a bread roll. "And who let it out."

Glenda snorted. "Huddle told you. It was the Trolls."

"They deny it and I believe them," Uncle Fitz immediately and predictably retorted. "And none of the other Monsters have opposable thumbs."

"Apart from Amelia, and Glenda" I corrected him. "But Amelia wouldn't leave the sauna even in a heatwave and Glenda wouldn't waste the energy."

Glenda rapped me on the heated with the soup ladle. "Are you calling me lazy, young man?" She then sizzled and spat at the Simpkins. "Would anyone else like to comment?"

"No," said Joss. "Not whilst you're holding that metal spoon."

"I've an idea," I said, addressing the Simpkins. "I'll come back to your house with you to get your stuff and we'll ask people in the village if they know anything." I reached for the butter. "Huddle will have told the entire population about the Gremlin."

"Good plan," Joss said. "We can cycle back here. You can use my old bike, Kade."

Grosse Village was old, small and quaint. Or decrepit and ready to be demolished. Depended on your point of view. It consisted of a long, narrow, zig-zagging High Street with several more chaotic lanes straggling off it. Its gothic, timber-framed houses and shops, most of them leaning at alarming angles, suggested that nothing new had been built in the last several hundred years. The place had the appearance of being frozen in time. Unlike the news of the Gremlin. Gossip flew as fast as the ring of tethered bats circling the chimney pots of the slanty roof cottage next door to the Simpkins' house. I followed the twins and Ivy, curious to see inside. To my astonishment the interior was as modern as its outside was ancient.

"Mum!" Dancing into the open-plan kitchen diner, Ivy addressed a pair of feet protruding from underneath the sink. Mrs Simpkins slid out on one of those trolley glide things used by mechanics, a wrench gripped in one hand and a wet football sock covered in gooey yuck in the other.

"Hello, Ivy," she said, followed by, "which of you two boys blocked the waste disposal with this?" She brandished the sock at her sons.

"Harsh," Joss said to his mum in an injured voice. "How do you know it's not Ivy's?"

"She doesn't wear football socks and knows the purpose of a laundry basket."

Joss considered this. "Fair call."

"It's mine," Calvin said. "I left it by the sink with the dirty plates and must've confused it with Dad's homemade lasagne when I cleared up. Sorry. Can we stay at Kade's tonight?"

Sock mystery solved Mrs Simpkins flashed a smile in

my direction. "Hello, Kade. Thank you for asking my trio over. They're Monster mad."

"No worries," I said, silently thanking Uncle Fitz for pretending that the invite had been my idea, rather than making me look desperate by him having to find me friends.

"Can we go?" Impatient, Ivy jiggled about.

"Yes." Mrs Simpkins got back to work under the sink.

"Come on." Joss shepherded me towards the stairs. At the top, Ivy skipped off into her room whilst I went with the twins to theirs. However, as soon as I walked in, I practically threw myself out again. A three metre long dragon clung to the ceiling space; claws implanted in the wooden rafters. Neck twisted so that it looked down on whoever was entering, it stared unblinkingly.

"Realistic isn't it?" said Joss. "Brother Ben's handiwork. If you tug its tail, it roars and spits out fire. Or at least it did before Mum got hold of it."

"We accidentally set light to the curtains," Calvin explained, dropping down onto the lower of two bunkbeds. "But the Boggart-Under-The-Floor still works." He clapped his hands. A heart-stopping shriek blasted out from beneath the rug. The edges shifted as a long, waggling, red tongue snaked out from between two floorboards and shot towards my ankles. The movement was accompanied by a manic and scarily realistic giggle.

"We have a safe below that spot," Calvin continued, "where we stash our special stuff. Like the boots Ben made, with built-in GPS."

As the Simpkins were sharing their secrets with me, I felt that now was the moment to share back. Especially as there was no chance of Uncle Fitz overhearing.

"I've something to tell you," I said, sitting on a giant beanbag. "Can you call Ivy in?

"What for?" On cue, Ivy appeared in the doorway clutching a backpack. She kicked the door shut with her heel. "Go on then," she said with a nod at me.

"Promise to keep it to yourselves," I said. "And not tell your parents or my uncle. I don't want Huddle finding out."

"We promise." Calvin spoke for all three.

I lowered my voice. "I know who the prowler is. It's Mr Worthington."

The twins' mouths fell open. Ivy's too. And she didn't even go to Grosse High!

"Psycho Man?" Clearly, Ivy's brothers had provided a flawless description.

Yes. Him," I said, going on to tell them everything that had happened in the wood and school. By the end, the Simpkins' jaws were almost smacking the floor.

"It's outrageous. I know there's a teacher shortage, but what kind of nutjobs are schools employing?" Joss said. "I think we should report him. I can understand why you don't want Huddle involved, but we could call Scotland Yard."

"No." I shook my head. "They'd take the Monsters away. And Uncle Fitz. I think that'd finish him off. It's why I've not told him about Mr Worthington. That and the fact that I don't want to end up in care. You won't tell, will you?" I cast the Simpkins an anxious look and received three offended ones back. Ivy spoke up.

"Of course not. We couldn't help solve the mystery of the Phantom Prowler if we did."

"Kade's already solved it," Joss pointed out.

"Now it's a case of what to do," I said. "And of finding the Gremlin." I stood up. "Let's start now with the village."

As I'd predicted, Huddle had been out and about,

telling people to stay away from the Gremlin if they saw it and to keep all doors and windows locked. The villagers, although Uncle Fitz swore blind to their loyalty, weren't happy about the situation. There was plenty of talk.

"The Gremlin's disappeared," a woman with long, jangly earrings told a young mother pushing a double buggy over the cracked cobblestones. "Either ran away or was taken."

"I hope for taken," the mother said, shaking her head of wild, curly hair until it seemed alive. "I've heard it's vicious. I don't want my little twins getting bitten." She gave her toddlers a soppy smile. The two small, slightly scary looking girls ignored her. They were busy worrying their soft toys with the same kind of wild dog-like determination that the Gremlin employed. I didn't think their mother needed to worry. Her little darlings looked more than capable of defending themselves. One of them locked eyes with me and growled.

Up and down the streets, opinion about the Gremlin varied.

"Poor little thing," the woman who ran the bakery told me, ringing up the price of a banana loaf on an antiquated till that was too old even for a museum. "I know it has a nasty reputation, but I don't like to think of it being lost. I wonder where it is?"

One of her customers muttered that Mars wouldn't be far enough.

These two attitudes were pretty typical. Some people were sympathetic, whilst others were with the bakery customer. But even so, they didn't seem the type to act on it. Their close-knit community really did include the manor, and there was a shared concern that if a stranger found the Gremlin, it might mean repercussions for everyone.

"Perhaps it'll come back on its own," Calvin said as we cycled up to the Manor gates. "Sooner or later it's going to get hungry. *Careful!*" He swerved as Victor swung the car out of the driveway. Calvin's bike hit mine. I crashed into Joss, who took out Ivy. We all toppled to the ground, sandwiched between the bikes. The car stopped. Uncle Fitz stuck his head out of the window. Behind the wheel, Victor smirked.

Ivy whispered in my ear. "I think Victor's determined to take me out and doesn't care about collateral damage. Don't worry, I'll get our own back for us."

"Sorry. Can't imagine how Victor didn't see you," Uncle Fitz apologised, unaware of the covert battle at play between Ivy and his chauffeur. "Did you learn anything in the village about my Gremlin, Kade? Glenda and Victor helped me search the house and grounds again whilst you were out; it's definitely not here. Victor and I are going on a wider search."

"We'll come with you," I offered.

Uncle Fitz shook his head. "I need you here in case the Gremlin comes back. Oh," he added. "I've ordered your new Smartphone. Mr Simpkins has a meeting in Truro tomorrow so he's going to collect it. It's an XPhone 12..."

"*XPhone 12?*" I gaped.

"The X phone with the X Factor." Ivy quoted the manufacturer's slogan. "Costs mega bucks."

"He deserves it," Uncle Fitz said. He's a big help to me. And I know how he really feels about my work, even if he does pretend to complain. Remember how good you were with that aqua phobic Mermaid, Kade, when you were five? You had her swimming again in no time." Uncle Fitz glowed at the memory. "You may be Jones by name but you're a Withershins by nature. Oh, and feed the dog, will you? And the Shapeshifter," he added as Victor started the car up again, this time almost taking Calvin with him.

We pedalled up the long, tree-lined driveway. The closer to the house we got, the louder grew the noise of what sounded like a pack of deranged dingoes. It was Me, Myself and I howling for his dinner and walkies. The front doors shuddered as inside the dog launched himself at them. We decided we'd go around the back instead.

Through the kitchen window, we could see Glenda doing the washing up. She was wearing ear defenders. The Banshee raised soapy hands as we came in.

"Take that flipping dog out. His barking's driving me nuts!" she snapped.

"Ivy and I'll walk him," Calvin offered. "Where's his lead?"

"In the pantry," I said. "Joss can help me feed the Shapeshifter whilst you're out."

Glenda handed me a blue plastic tub from the fridge.

"For the Shapeshifter?" Joss asked. "As it was a mouse the last time I saw it, I bet I know what's in there."

"Bet you don't," I answered. "In this place nothing's as it seems."

"It's plain pasta," Glenda said, sniffing. "The hoity-toity creature insists on Italian food. That it's adding to my workload doesn't matter of course."

Me, Myself and I, who'd given up on the front door, burst in. Seeing Calvin holding his lead he exploded into ecstatic barks and leapt, intent on delivering a whole package of huge, slurpy kisses. Calvin keeled over. Joss and I hurried off, leaving Ivy to rescue her brother before he could change his mind about who should take Me, Myself and I for a walk.

Uncle Fitz had made a home for the Shapeshifter in a

small storage room built into one of the attic's eaves. All the clobber, including the carpet, had been evicted.

"Your uncle said that the fewer furnishings the better," Joss said. "He called it the minimalistic approach. All that's left inside are things that can't be removed. Like the walls. Hey, that's cool! The Shapeshifter's being all arty. It looks like something painted by that Spanish bloke with the droopy moustache. You know – Salvador Dali."

The Shapeshifter was posing as a window melting into the floorboards. POP! Noting our arrival, it added hands to its appearance. Spotting the food tub, the Monster slithered over, sniffling puppy fashion. A second POP cracked the air; the Shapeshifter added Joss's head to its collective shape. It rammed a handful of pasta into its mouth. I snatched the tub out of reach.

"Manners," I said. The Shapeshifter burped. I gave it a pat and doled out a small portion of food on to the tub's lid. "Go slow or you'll give yourself indigestion."

Joss watched me refilling the makeshift plate. "Can I try?"

"Sure. Go ahead." I handed Joss the tub, but the Monster protested. I patted it again.

Joss handed the tub back. "Seriously, mate," he said, as the Shapeshifter lay on its back, purring, "I have to agree with your uncle. You do like Monsters more than you say."

"Maybe," I admitted, standing up. The Shapeshifter, now in the form of the overhead light bulb, went to sleep. From below Amelia's singing floated up.

"Should we check on her?" Joss asked.

"No." I shook my head. "That's her falling asleep song."

"Really?" Joss said, intrigued.

"Yes. It means she's stoked up her coal and is heading for the Land of Dreams."

Joss gave me an admiring grin. "Mate, you're a natural at this job. Why don't you want to inherit the place?" Getting no answer, he probed deeper. "Is it to do with your mum?"

I took a sharp breath, my grip on the tub tightened. "What do you know about that?"

"Cool it, dude," Joss raised his hands. "Breathe and count to ten. Here, give me the tub. Your knuckles are going white." He wrestled the tub away from me. "Sir Fitz is friends with my gran. She told us that your mum loved the Monsters. Before your dad brought her here, she'd thought the sole place left to discover amazing creatures was in the sea. She was a marine biologist like him, wasn't she? Didn't he meet her in St Lucia rescuing baby turtles?"

"Why ask?" I snapped, trying to snatch the tub back. "You seem to know the story."

"Fine." Joss held the container out of reach. Being two years older he had a height advantage. "Gran said that before your dad brought your mum here, he made her a bet. If he showed her a land animal that could blow her mind more than the strangest sea-creature, then she'd marry him. And she did. They lived here when they weren't working on marine projects. You were born here. Gran was your mum's midwife. She delivered you."

"Really?" I said in a tone that dripped acid rain. But Joss failed to dissolve.

"Yeah, Gran says you were the ugliest baby ever." He gave a serious nod. "Uglier than her next-door neighbour's kids and they make the Gremlin look stunning."

"*What?*" Joss's gran was a rude old bat! "She said what? That's so not true!"

Joss erupted in howls of laughter. He slapped my shoulder. "Course it's not! I'm joking. I was trying to relieve the tension. Humour's a good way."

"My mum used to say that," I said. "But she died. Here. And that wasn't funny at all."

"True," Joss replied. "But at least she died somewhere she loved."

I didn't know how to answer that, so I changed the subject. "You're pretty keen on Uncle Fitz's line of work. Perhaps you should do it."

"I wish," Joss said. "Calvin and Ivy too. What do you want to do, then? Be a detective? You were good at noticing everything Huddle missed."

"It wasn't difficult," I said, glad to move off the subject of Mum. "But yes. However, I'm down for babysitting Uncle Fitz's pets."

Joss let out another hoot of laughter. "Sorry," he apologised, noting my sour expression. "But I'd hardly call looking after Monsters babysitting. Not unless the babies have massive behaviour issues. And finding them *does* need detective skills. Do you think you just walk out into the back of beyond shouting, 'Hey Monster, come to Daddy?' Don't think so."

I found Joss's pep talk highly suspect. "What are you getting at?"

"Umm." Joss fiddled with his tie. "When Dad suggested we get to know you, a certain... *thought*... did occur."

"Such as?" I said, adjusting the lid of the Shapeshifter's food tub with a sharp snap.

Joss hurried on. "We thought that if we got on, then perhaps we could work here too. After all, we practically *are* Monsters give or take a few generations. Who'd be better? And look how good we've been at teamwork so far. It's like we've known each other for years."

True. We'd clicked. Like I'd clicked with Arnie on our first day at secondary school. Sometimes, that happened. The Simpkins reminded me of Arnie. They were fun.

"You could be the leg-man," Joss said. "Find Monsters and bring them back. You could be The Great Monster Detective. You could be," Joss flung out his arms. "Monster Holmes!"

"Or I could be a regular detective," I said.

"Or you could be a regular, boring detective," Joss agreed, dropping his arms. "No problem. You ignore the endangered animals' crisis; ignore that you could help."

"I'll think about it," I said. "But really, it's up to Uncle Fitz. Does the deal involve Ivy? She can be a bit scary."

"You think she's a liability?" Calvin asked, looking concerned.

"No," I said. "I think she'd make a great security officer. You saw her with the Trolls."

It was several hours before Uncle Fitz came back to the Manor. During that time, once we had the Monsters settled for the night, we held a meeting in the sitting room about Mr Worthington.

"We need to put him under surveillance," I said. "And confirm what his objective is."

"You could nick his phone and hack it like he did yours," Ivy suggested.

I shook my head. "Too risky. But we could do an online search and see if anything comes up about him."

But Mr Worthington's digital footprint was non-existent. We couldn't find anything, no matter how hard we tried. He didn't seem to have any social media accounts and didn't feature at all on the school website beyond the staff list. But I wasn't giving up.

"Don't suppose your brother's given you any bugging devices or trackers?" I asked the Simpkins. "Something tiny that we could plant on Mr Worthington, first day back at school."

"No, but we can ask Ben to send us something," Calvin said.

Glenda stuck her head round the door. "Why aren't you lot in bed? It's late."

"We're waiting for Uncle Fitz to come back," I said.

"He is back; without the Gremlin and very tired and upset too. See?" She flung back the door to show Uncle Fitz standing in the hallway hanging up his jacket.

"I've found nothing," he replied, in answer to our questions. "No sign of my Gremlin anywhere." Gloom spilt out of him. He looked weary and old. I felt sorry for him.

"You go to bed," I said. "We'll wait up in case the Gremlin comes back."

But it didn't. The thing had vanished like an evaporated puddle.

"Perhaps the prowler did nick it." Ivy yawned as the hours slid towards midnight. "Or maybe it's out having a nice time on the moors terrorising sheep."

"Then I pity them. They're already traumatised from Victor's driving," I said. "Let's hope that no farmers see it and think it's their worst nightmare come true."

"Talking of which, can we watch *Is it Real? You Tell Me!*" Joss asked eagerly. "It's my favourite reality programme."

"He fancies the presenter, Angel LeBlanc," Calvin informed me.

Joss stuck his nose in the air. "I admire the way she angles the show. Real talent."

I didn't agree. Angel LeBlanc was a tall, flashy blonde who encouraged viewers to ring in with stories of weird creature sightings. She spent all her time racing about, first banging on that stories of creepy beasties haunting the area were true and then totally debunking them. The show wasn't scary at all. Except when people didn't do what Angel wanted.

But that night Grosse Village had its own scary encounter. Burglaries. Destructive break-ins with whole houses vandalised. But the thief left prints. Not fingerprints, because the thief didn't appear to have fingers, but definite marks. They also left an erratic but easy to follow trail of scattered pieces. And where did it lead? *To Grosse Manor of course!* But, early next morning, when Huddle's police car rushed up the drive, siren wailing and lights flashing, waking us all up from where we'd fallen asleep in the sitting room, Uncle Fitz neither heard nor saw. He was too busy dancing for joy. For there, curled up snoring in its nest, lay the Gremlin. And around its neck hung a jewellery store's worth of necklaces.

"Now," said a puzzled Uncle Fitz, "how on earth has it got hold of *those?*"

Chapter 6

Deck the Hall with Stolen Property

Huddle had a theory for why the Gremlin had dressed itself up as a bling Christmas tree. It involved Uncle Fitz. And Huddle had no intention of letting friendship interfere with duty. Uncle Fitz looked like his best friend had morphed into his worst enemy. I felt dead sorry for him. That Gremlin always caused trouble.

"It's no good going on about how long we've known each other, Fitz," Huddle said as he scribbled away in his notebook. "The law's the law and your Gremlin's broken it."

Uncle Fitz was almost crying. "But it's not the Gremlin's fault; it's just a little animal. You can't blame it for its actions." He wrung his hands in despair.

"I'm not." Huddle produced a pair of handcuffs. "I'm blaming you. Like you say, the Gremlin's an animal. As it's keeper, you're top of my suspect list. I'm arresting you on suspicion of aggravated robbery and grand theft." He clicked the handcuffs around Uncle Fitz's wrists.

"That's not fair!" I said, angry at Huddle's attitude. "Uncle Fitz might have strange ideas, but they don't include thinking that other people's stuff is his. He's been set up!"

"How do you know that?" Cross at being questioned, Huddle stuck his lower lip out.

"Because he was here all night," I said. "And there's..." I did a quick count up, "five witnesses to that. Joss call your dad. It's time for a lawyer."

"On it," Joss said, whipping out his phone. Unluckily for Uncle Fitz, the line was busy. "He mustn't have finished his meeting in Truro. Don't worry, I'll leave a voice mail." Joss shot Huddle a sassy look. "Dad, call me, Sir Fitz needs you. Huddle's arrested him."

"It's Chief Constable to you," said Huddle. "And Sir Fitz can call from jail. Come on, Fitz, you know the law; 'guilty until proven innocent'."

"It's the other way around!" I bellowed, throwing up my hands. "How can you not *know* that?"

"I'm innocent!" Uncle Fitz wailed. "It's the truth. What else can I *say?*"

"Worst day ever?" suggested Ivy. Followed by, "Ouch!" as Calvin kicked her.

Huddle remained unmoved. The Gremlin for its part slept on. It must've been exhausted from all its dirty deeds because usually it detected visitors before they arrived. It rolled over, releasing a slow flow of dribble. Two earrings slid out from the side of its mouth.

Huddle cleared his throat. "I think a search of its nest is in order." The search produced three diamond bracelets and a half-eaten burger. Huddle coughed and ticked an item off his 'reported stolen' list. "I'm going to have to examine the rest of the house."

Bad news for Uncle Fitz. The Gremlin had jazzed up the entire Manor with its loot.

"This makes seven rooms so far," I hissed at Joss as Huddle took a photograph of a hat stand colourfully decked with jewellery, watches and other dangly bits of 'acquired' pieces.

Investigation of Uncle Fitz's study led to the further discovery of wads of cash, twenty smartphones, thirty tablets, an infinite number of watches and four packets of biscuits. The Gremlin had put its multiple limbs to good use. But even so, the amount of stuff?

"The Gremlin couldn't have carried all this," I said. "Not even with all its tentacles. It obviously had help."

Huddle didn't take this the way I meant – that the wretched thing had had help from *outside* the Manor. He sucked in his lips. "Which is why I'm arresting your uncle. Nobody else can get near that Gremlin."

"But I've already told you," I said through gritted teeth. "It couldn't be him."

Uncle Fitz, wild-eyed and desperate, nodded agreement until his head almost fell off. But Huddle wasn't having it. "So you say," he said tucking away his notebook. "For all I know you're making it up." So, despite our protests, Uncle Fitz was bundled into the police car and driven off to jail. Glenda tried to foil the proceedings by screeching into Huddle's ear.

"Stop that, Glenda, or I'll arrest you too for disturbance of the peace," Huddle snapped, leaving the Banshee standing on the front steps groaning and wringing her hands.

Uncle Fitz stuck his head out of the window as the

vehicle trundled off. "Kade, take care of my Monsters; I'm relying on *yoooouuu!*"

"Bet Sir Fitz wishes he knew where the Gremlin hid the gate fobs," Ivy said. "Huddle wouldn't have been able to get in."

Glenda wailed again. This time an octave higher. A slate fell from the roof.

"Come on." Calvin took her arm before she could draw another breath. "Let's go and park you someplace you can have a nice rest, and nobody has to hear you." He led her inside.

I continued staring after the car, fists clenched. "Uncle Fitz is innocent." I swung round on Joss and Ivy. "I'm going to clear his name."

"*We're* going to clear his name," Joss corrected. "We're your mates. It's going to be a hard job though. Huddle's clearly set his heart on having someone behind bars."

"Yeah, we'll have to give him somebody else" Ivy said. "You volunteer, Joss."

But I'd already decided who it'd be. Mr Worthington. Whether he'd been here to snoop, kidnap or had released the Gremlin by accident, Uncle Fitz's arrest was all its fault.

"Guys," I said to Joss and Ivy, "we're going to give Huddle, Mr Worthing..."

"**YOOOOW!**" An unholy screeching like a mad cat shattered the end of my sentence.

"Sorry," Joss apologised. "My mobile." He drew it out of his pocket, read the screen and then addressed Ivy. "It's Mum. Hey, Mum, you won't believe what's happened. Sir Fitz..."

Mrs Simpkins' voice, loud and exasperated, spilled

out of the phone as an *I-so-don't- believe-this* look filled Joss's face. He lowered the phone. "Ivy, we have to go home. Our house is one of those that the Gremlin visited, and it may have helped itself to a few things. Mum's not happy that Dad went off to Truro, leaving her to clear up."

"Sorry," I mouthed, feeling that an apology was owed. After all, the Gremlin lived here.

"Not your fault, mate," Joss said. Followed by, "Yes, Mum, I *am* listening."

I didn't know what Mrs Simpkins was saying, but I hoped I wasn't being held responsible for the Gremlin's light fingers.

Joss ended the call. "Mum's messaging Dad about your uncle and said to tell you not to worry, because nobody's blaming him. Though I don't think people feel quite the same way towards the Gremlin," he added. "Ivy, go and tell Calvin what's happened. We'll call you later, Kade. I'll leave you my phone so it's easier to keep in touch."

"You know where we are if you need us," Calvin said as we peddled down the driveway.

"Thanks," I said. "But don't worry. The Gremlin's banged up, and the other Monsters aren't a problem. Apart from the Trolls that is, but the trick there's to avoid them whenever possible."

We'd taken advantage of the Gremlin's catatonic state to shift it to a different, windowless room with a door that had six bolts plus a nice, solid lock. To stop the Gremlin getting bored, I'd put in a basket of chew toys, plus its portable gymnastic bars for exercise.

"Bit of a change of heart, then," Ivy commented. "So

far you've given the impression that you prefer toothache. But, at least you're trying."

Calvin gave Ivy a teasing smile. "Wow, Ivy. From you that's almost a compliment."

"He's an only, so I've decided to adopt him," Ivy answered, practising her wheelies as she sailed through the gates. "It'll make you and Joss have to work harder for my attention."

Back at the house, Glenda hadn't ceased her wailing, with Me, Myself and I joining in with the highest notes. I flopped down onto the porch steps and tried to devise a strategy for getting Uncle Fitz out of jail and Mr Worthington in. But I needed to prove his motive. Was Mr Worthington a secret Monster Collector himself and therefore a jealous rival? I dismissed this. Our Year 7 Residential Trip had included a visit to Paignton Zoo's Crocodile Swamp. Mr Worthington, after taking one look at its weird (but at least recognisable) inhabitants, had denounced them as the most blindingly, hideous creatures he'd ever seen and anybody who thought different needed their brain tested. Did Mr Worthington think he'd a public duty to stop Uncle Fitz from populating Cornwall with even stranger critters? But then, why bother nicking the Gremlin when there were easier ways to grass up Uncle Fitz, like posting the photos on social media?

The most likely motive of course was profit. The Monsters were valuable. Amelia would be worth a fortune to a private animal collector or a scientific research lab. I bit my bottom lip. Yes, profit was the obvious answer. But how could I prove it without evidence as hard to miss as the Great Wall of China? I needed something that Mr Worthington wouldn't be able to wriggle out of. Like a recording of his threatening behaviour in the classroom. I wished I'd thought of that at the time. But it wouldn't have been possible anyhow as the stupid Gremlin had drowned my phone. But once I was back in school I'd be ready. If Ben couldn't provide us with a bugging device, I'd record Mr Worthington on my new phone demanding his daily report. If that wasn't rock solid evidence, then nothing was. I found myself wishing it wasn't half term. Uncle Fitz was facing eight more days locked away. Perhaps Mr Simpkins could arrange bail? He was Uncle Fitz's lawyer after all. I'd call him once he'd had time to get home from Truro.

I was surprised to realise that I was already missing the Simpkins. The place felt quiet (human quiet that is; Glenda and the dog were still baying like mad hyenas) without their banter. Behind me, I could hear the babbling water from the fountain, clattering down into the huge basin where long ago I'd given the aqua phobic Mermaid her swimming lessons. The Mermaid had been American. Each time I'd passed, she'd erupted from the water, soaking all and everything as she high fived me, yelling "Yo, bro! You're the man!" Until she'd returned 'Stateside', the porch had been one huge puddle.

I hadn't thought about the Mermaid in, well, forever. Or any of the Monsters I'd helped Uncle Fitz with. Like the Winged Horse with vertigo. I'd resolved her altitude issues by catapulting apples sky-high until her love of eating proved greater than her fear of heights. Uncle Fitz had given me a badge for this, reading: 'Second-In-Command'. I'd worn it proudly.

Then Mum had died.

Mum had been the Monsters biggest fan – Gremlin excepted because not even she, who'd excused a shark that'd tried to eat her, could find anything nice to say about it. The week after my sixth birthday, she and Dad had flown off to join an Amazonian River Expedition where they'd met an Encantado (a friendly Water Monster resembling the Pink River Dolphins native to that part of the Amazon) that had become obsessed with the music from a riverside village fiesta. The creature had set up a one Monster fan club, refusing to leave and annoying the locals by eating all their fish. My parents had stayed on until they'd managed to persuade him to swim away by gifting him a pair of maracas.

Mum had come back feeling very tired. She'd blamed it on jetlag. But weeks later, nothing had changed. Eventually, Dad had made her see a doctor who'd asked some questions before rushing her to a hospital for Tropical Diseases. Mum'd contracted a rare virus, peculiar to the region where the Encantado had discovered its love of music. Little by little, she'd faded away, sleeping more and more until one morning she didn't wake up. I'd run into the bedroom with a bunch of her favourite flowers fresh from the garden to find Dad crying, Mum's hand limp in his. I remember a long silence that said nothing and everything. I remember throwing the flowers down and running from the room, straight into Uncle Fitz, who'd held me tight. His waistcoat had smelt of peppermint and Gremlin.

After that, things had moved fast. The funeral. Dad sorting out Mum's things. Although as quickly as he'd packed them, I'd unpacked them again, not able to understand how Mum could be dead. But what I had understood was that it was that musically challenged Encantado's fault. If Mum hadn't met it, she'd be alive. Stupid Monsters. The next time Uncle Fitz had asked for help with his latest problem ridden creature I'd told him to get lost!

Soon, I'd become totally anti-Monster. And showed it. After I'd water-boarded the Gremlin with the garden hose because it'd played vampires with my paddling pool, Uncle Fitz had told Dad that I had 'unresolved issues' and that some 'thinking time' away might help. He'd encouraged Dad to take me with him on a research job in the Mediterranean.

We'd spent two, amazing months at sea with no reminders of Mum and no Monsters. At the end of the project, we'd moved on to the South of France for further work and then to London where Dad had presented a series of lectures at the Natural History Museum. When he'd finally suggested it was time to go back to Grosse Manor, I'd thrown the mother of all tantrums until he promised that we'd never go back. And we hadn't. Until now. Now I was back where I'd started. It was what Mum used to call 'full circle'. And if this happened, Mum had always believed it was for a reason.

I blinked. Blimey! If this was true, then it meant I was *supposed* to be here; Uncle Fitz had said that by nature I was a Withershins. This meant I belonged at Grosse Manor. If I hadn't been obsessed with feeling sorry for myself, Mr Worthington would never have got his mitts on my phone and none of this would have happened. A sudden – very rare – emotion swamped me. GUILT. I could so easily be the person Uncle Fitz believed I was. In that moment I made a solemn promise not to let him down. My gaze fell on Me, Myself and I standing a short distance away. He'd abandoned Glenda and was now eating grass. The last time he'd snacked on the lawn he'd been stupendously sick over the kitchen floor. I stood up. At this present time I might not be able to prove Uncle Fitz's innocence, but I did have a plan, and meantime. I could do something else to help him. I could get on with taking care of the Monsters. Starting with stopping Me, Myself and I thinking he was a herbivore.

A couple of hours later, when I'd finished cleaning up after the dog who'd thrown up from his experiment with vegetarianism, and I'd finished clipping Old Smokey's toenails, Joss's mobile rang. I was tidying Amelia's room. Startled by the yowling, the Yeti whipped round, her wide, purple eyes searching for the non-existent cat. With a stubby, quivering finger, she gave my pocket a suspicious prod. The phone slipped out, landing with a clatter on the floor. From its screen, Calvin grinned out. Amelia ogled him in wonder. I could tell she was thinking that he'd been a lot bigger the last time she'd seen him.

"No worries," I said, picking up the gadget. It's Calvin facetiming." Amelia shambled across and peered over my shoulder. "Sorry, she got to it first," I said.

Calvin grinned. "For a minute I thought you'd aged eighty years and needed a haircut."

"Ha, ha, very funny," I said. "Is your dad there? I want to talk to him about setting bail for Uncle Fitz. I've been researching it and Huddle's not in a position to refuse." (I'd been surfing Law websites online whilst seeing to the Monsters. I'm good at multi-tasking.)

"Dad's with Huddle," Calvin said. "Don't worry, his success rate is ninety-nine-point-nine per cent. He's a brilliant negotiator. His methods even work on Ivy."

An ominous rumble cut into our conversation, followed by a tremendous crash as if something had hit the ground at high speed.

"What was *that?*" I asked.

Calvin's expression clouded. "Our Gaming System. The Gremlin stuck it on the roof."

"That Gremlin owes a lot of people apologies," I said.

"Mum says she'll throttle it if it comes within a five-mile radius." Calvin angled the phone to show a defeated, ripped, upside-down sofa and a coffee table minus three of its legs. "It also scribbled over Ivy's school photo. But that's nothing compared to next door. You should see what the Gremlin left in their bathroom. Did you know it isn't potty trained? It scoffed their tropical fish too."

I winced. "Sorry."

"Oh, no worries, mate. Nobody's blaming you or Sir Fitz," Calvin said. "Although I can't say the same about the Gremlin. People keep calling and asking if Ben can invent an Anti-Gremlin spray. Hold on, Mum wants me."

I had close-up of the sitting room carpet as Calvin held the phone upside down. There was a gabbled exchange during which his voice noticeably rose.

"What? Huddle said what? I can't tell him that!"

Mrs Simpkins' voice said something that sounded like, "You'll have to."

Calvin resumed our conversation. "Mate, I hate to tell you this, but... you know how I said that Dad succeeds ninety-nine-point-nine per cent of the time?"

"Ye..es?" I said, not liking where this seemed to be going.

"Sir Fitz is in the point-one percent fail category. I'm really sorry, Kade, but it looks like Huddle's not letting him go anytime soon."

I felt faint. Everything went blurry as Calvin's voice faded out to be once more replaced by **DAH, DAH, DAAAH!!**

"Kade?" Calvin's anxious voice finally reached me. "You okay? Look, I'm sure Dad will sort things out. I'll call you later when I've spoken to him."

"I'm not waiting until later," I said, furious with Huddle. "I'm coming over now."

The Simpkins were also fuming. They'd taken their dad's failure very personally. They sat disgusted around the kitchen table, arms tightly folded. My new XPhone lay in its box in front of me, complete with the latest accessories. Unfortunately, due to the circumstances, I couldn't feel as pleased with it as I'd have liked.

"We don't get it," Joss said. "I mean, your uncle's not one of Britain's Most Wanted."

"Maybe somebody's putting pressure on Huddle," Ivy said, chewing the end of her plaits. "Ooh, do you think he's being blackmailed by Mr Worthington?"

"No," I said. "I think he's very stubborn."

"At least we'll be prepared if Mr Worthington pays Grosse Manor another visit," Joss said. Having decided that it was necessary to be prepared for this scenario, I'd asked the Simpkins if I could borrow a range of Ben's anti-burglar inventions so we could secure the grounds. My next move was to go and see Uncle Fitz. I wanted to tell him my plans so that he'd know the Monsters were safe.

"Come on guys," I said. "We're going to see my uncle."

Chapter 7

The Return of Aunt Hildegarde

At the station, Uncle Fitz lounged on a comfy armchair in the back room eating biscuits with Huddle and laughing at something on the T.V. Although I'd never been arrested, I was pretty sure this wasn't standard procedure. There was something odd going on.

"Unusual police cell," I said, noting the fussy little side-tables and stripy scatter rugs. Someone had picked out a matching pattern for the sofa and armchair cushions. A large, framed photo of Huddle at the beach with his wife and grandchildren hung on the wall.

"My wife made the room cosy because I spend so much time here," Huddle said.

"And Eric's kindly letting me use it," Uncle Fitz added.

"Shouldn't you be in a cell if Chief Constable Huddle thinks you're a dangerous crim?" I asked. "Instead of enjoying T.V. and sharing biscuits?"

"We're old friends," Huddle said. "No need for formalities like the cells."

"Particularly as Auntie Jane's in there painting flowers on the walls." A young officer breezed in and handed Uncle Fitz a mug of tea. I guessed this must be Huddle's nephew, Joe.

Huddle glared at him. "Haven't you got reports to write up, Joe?"

"Yes Sir!" Joe saluted and marched from the room. Huddle stared crossly after him.

"Uncle Fitz," I said, getting straight to the point, "why've you been refused bail?"

Uncle Fitz blushed. "Wee...ell, it's a matter of protocol. Bit difficult to explain, but Eric knows I'm innocent. Now, now, Kade, it's not how it seems." Seeing me shoot Huddle a hostile glare, Uncle Fitz came to his friend's rescue. "It's a ruse. We've teamed up to catch whoever did free the Gremlin."

Ha! I knew it. There was something funny going on.

Huddle glowed. "The real culprit will think they're safe, unaware that I'm investigating them." His entire being gleamed with satisfaction. The fact that he didn't know who the real culprit *was*, seemed to have escaped him. For his part, Uncle Fitz appeared happy to go along with Huddle.

"You don't mind do you, Kade? I mean it's not as if you're home alone." Uncle Fitz sipped his tea. "There's Glenda to keep the house ticking over. She's quite capable you know."

Wrong. Once she'd finished howling, Glenda had announced that she had a migraine and was off to bed. She'd added that it was likely she was coming down with a bad case of 'nerves,' which would render her incapable of any type of work, including cooking.

"Kade can always stay with us," Joss offered. "Mum won't mind."

Uncle Fitz almost choked on his mouthful of tea. *"But what about my Monsters?"*

"Or we'll stay with Kade." Joss backtracked, realising his offer hadn't ben appreciated.

"Yes, yes, good thinking," Uncle Fitz wheezed, wiping his moustache. "Go and ask your parents. No don't phone." (Joss had whipped out his mobile.) "In person is better."

"Gotcha," said Joss. "Strength in numbers. Let's go, guys." He hustled his brother and sister away. From outside the room, a phone began a shrill, nagging ring. Huddle humphed.

"Why isn't Joe answering that?" he said, stomping off to take the call.

Uncle Fitz seized my arm. "Kade, listen, there's something I've not told Eric because, well, as you've seen he's a nice chap but..."

"Not exactly Brainiac?" I supplied.

"I wasn't going to put it quite that way," Uncle Fitz said, "but yes. He's put Beryl our local traffic warden at the top of his suspects list. Eric cautioned her recently for putting parking tickets on toddlers' pedal cars. He thinks it could be her revenge by making extra work for him. It's nonsense of course. Beryl has several witnesses to her clamping cars at the time."

"So who do you think did it?" I asked.

Uncle Fitz snuck a furtive look at the furniture as if it

might be listening. He lowered his voice. "*I believe it was my brother, your Uncle Clive who took the Gremlin.* I need your help to prove it without Eric knowing we're doing our own investigation and getting all upset.

"Why would your own brother set you up?" I asked, puzzled.

"Financial reasons," Uncle Fitz answered. "That letter you saw this morning was the latest in a series from him, asking for help in paying off some very big debts. He owes several rather disreputable characters a substantial amount of money."

"How much?" If Clive thought Uncle Fitz was loaded, he was going to be disappointed!

"Too much to pay back on his own." Uncle Fitz's shoulders sagged. His whole body spelt out gloom. "Clive wants me to sell the Monsters. I ignore his letters, but he continues to write, each time more desperate. I think he'll do anything. He has before. It's how I lost my foot. Clive vanished after Father disowned him for swapping Mother's jewellery for a yacht. When I opened my Rest Home, he arrived with Glenda and the Gremlin, saying he'd reformed and wanted to help. But his plan was to sell the Monsters and use the Gremlin as an instrument of crime. He tried to get rid of me by disguising a Nile Crocodile as a friendly Sea Dragon. My Monsters saved me." (At this point, I couldn't help stealing a peek at Uncle Fitz's foot.) "Yes." Uncle Fitz nodded. "The croc ate it. Clive hadn't fed the poor dear."

Wow. We had so much dirty history that our family could star in a reality show.

"Clive says he has us under surveillance." Uncle Fitz said, voice wobbling. He pulled out a silk handkerchief and blew his nose. "I should've listened to my sister: '*Rotten apples make terrible pies.*' As usual, she was spot on. Hildegarde's the one other person I've confided in. I wish she lived closer. You can't pop round to the Himalayas for a cup of tea and a chat about your worries. I know she'd see Clive's hand's in this. It would explain the Gremlin's escape. It'd go with him. It wouldn't realise he's rotten."

I didn't answer. My mind was already on information overload. *Under surveillance?* Bells, lights, buzzers; every alarm you can think of went off inside my head. The glove. Mr Worthington! Two crooks working together. Partners. It all made sense.

"Kade? Are you listening?" Uncle Fitz gave me a poke in the ribs. "If Clive thinks I'm under arrest, he's likely to target the Manor. I need you there when he does. We must protect the Monsters and our home. We can't let Clive win."

"We won't," I said, grabbing the chance to speak. "But there's something you need to know." I told him the whole saga, starting with the Gremlin's selfie. This was a huge mistake. Because the story involved his Little Darling, Uncle Fitz would *not* have it.

"The Gremlin started it all?" Uncle Fitz slapped on his 'I don't believe it,' expression. "My dear boy. You must stop being so negative about the Gremlin. Why would it take a selfie?"

"Because it's a little..."

"Ah, ah!" Uncle Fitz wagged a reproving finger. "Remember that it's my Gremlin who's the victim here. You're letting your frosty feelings towards it cloud your judgement. It's Clive who's at fault. As for an accomplice, it's clear my brother has someone working *for* if not *with* him, but what real evidence is there that it's your teacher?"

"The glove?" I said, trying not to sound annoyed.

"Lots of people share the same initials," Uncle Fitz said. "Eric can't charge a person over a glove. It's not *proof*. A wrong arrest could jeopardise everything."

"What about the other photos and the threats, then?" I challenged.

Uncle Fitz shook his head. "Well, you do have a very vivid imagination. Are you sure you're not overreacting to a telling off? Teachers are police checked you know."

As ever, Uncle Fitz insisted on innocent until proven guilty. He was forced to be anti- Clive because not even a braindead zombie could misinterpret somebody's intentions when they chucked you in front of a killer croc. I gave up. It was pointless arguing with him. I had to focus on the Monsters and getting Uncle Fitz released. Even though he wasn't exactly helping.

Seeing I'd caved, Uncle Fitz patted my arm. "Good man! Knew I could rely on you. Run along home now. My Monsters will need their supper. Collect your friends on the way."

This brought more bad news. Mrs Simpkins wouldn't let Ivy stay at the Manor. It was because of the stained dress, which she'd found buried in the wash basket.

"It was Glenda's fault," Ivy insisted. "Because she's a Banshee she likes drowning guests in whatever liquid she can get her hands on."

"Then nobody's going," Mrs Simpkins said. "Because Glenda's clearly unhinged."

"No she isn't," Calvin said, sending his sister a death ray glare. "Ivy's giving a heavily edited version of events."

"Honestly, it was an accident," I put in. "Please let her come."

Mrs Simpkins finally agreed. But that was because Ivy was driving her nuts.

Mr Simpkins offered to give us all a lift back to the

manor once he'd finished work, which gave me time to bring the Simpkins up to speed on the new info.

"Let's boobytrap the grounds tonight," I said. "Then we're prepared if Mr Worthington returns." I might have failed to convince Uncle Fitz about how sneaky Mr Worthington was, but Joss and Calvin having first-hand experience of him completely got it.

"We've already bagged up the goodies," Calvin said. "Wait till you see the digital, self-detaching tripwire. It locks itself around your legs and won't unlock without the code."

However, we'd no sooner piled into Mr Simpkins car, with our bikes safely attached, then the clouds burst open. The rain drummed down so heavily that it sounded like multiple steel bands trying to outplay each other.

"We'll have to wait until tomorrow to secure the grounds," I said, as blasts of water rebounded off the windows of Grosse Village's takeaway Pizza Palace. We'd stopped for takeaway as Glenda had made it clear not to expect any culinary delights from her.

Dropping us outside the manor, Mr Simpkins handed out the pizza boxes through the car window. "Here. Better get in before they dissolve. I'll see to the bikes."

Loaded up, we went off to feed the Monsters. Me, Myself and I, lured by the enticing aroma of hot dough and meaty toppings woke from his snooze and trailed after us in a drooling, semi-hypnotic trance. Ivy delivered Amelia's pizza to her (pepperoni with a double helping of red-hot chillies) but nobody wanted to play waiter to the Gremlin. We slid its supper under the door. Silence, then, **SPLAT**. Bits of blood red sauce sprayed out through the keyhole.

"It really is the most unlovable thing, isn't it?" Joss

picked bits of flayed tomato skin off his clothes. "No redeeming features whatsoever."

As the rain didn't stop, the Simpkins spent the next few hours checking Ben's devices whilst I downloaded a map of the grounds from GOOGLE Earth. I drew crosses on it indicating strategic places for the gadgets to be placed. After this, we went to bed. Ivy in the one prepared guestroom, whilst her brothers arranged sleeping bags on my floor. Exhausted, I was looking forward to getting some sleep but Joss, as I soon discovered, snored. Calvin fell asleep straight away, but then, he'd had fourteen years in which to get used to his brother's snorts.

Finally, my brain translated the staccato snores vibrating from Joss's airways into a dream. I was an F1 Driver, tearing up the track in front of a cheering crowd. Then, **_BANG! CRASH! THUMP!_** My car flipped over, smashing through the barriers. I woke with a start, but the banging, crashing and thumping continued. Someone was hammering on the front door.

"Who's that?" Joss poked a tousled head out of his sleeping bag. "How unsociable. What kind of person wakes you up at..." he squinted at his watch, "half-nine in the morning?"

He withdrew back into his cloth shell like an indignant tortoise. Meanwhile, Calvin slumbered on. As whoever it was showed no signs of leaving, I dragged myself out of bed and downstairs. The smell of toast hung in the air. Ivy, a loaf of bread under her arm, appeared. She reached the door first.

"Can I help you?"

The response wasn't in English. "Bildergardvithershins...cumtersi...my... bruderfits."

Ivy blinked. "Sorry, I didn't quite get that."

The visitor dumped a large carpetbag on the ground and tugged down the hood on their mega thick coat, ripping away several mouthfuls of woollen scarf. A head emerged.

"Sorry, old habit. Air's so chilly in the Himalayas that bundling up one's entire body becomes second nature. You soon develop a knack of knowing what's being chunted from behind multiple layers of llama wool. I'm Hildegarde Withershins, here to see my brother, Fitz. Who are you?"

"This is Ivy Simpkins," I said, stepping up. "And I'm Kade Jones. Sir Fitz is my uncle, so you must be my auntie."

Aunt Hildegarde considered this. "Nephew? Oh, you're the Jones boy. Tom's son's-daughter's-niece's-nephew's-brother's-child. Something like that. Knew I recognised the name. Fitz keeps me updated family wise. Births, marriages, etc." She paused. "Aren't you going to invite me in?"

I stepped back, yanking Ivy with me.

"Where is Fitz by the way?" Aunt Hildegarde peered up and down the hall.

"In jail," I said.

"*Jail?*" Aunt Hildegarde's tall body practically folded into a question mark. "Fitz? Why? He's always been so law-abiding." She paused. "Although he may take a few side-steps when it comes to his Monsters." Aunt Hildegarde clearly knew her brother.

"It's true," I said, closing the door behind her as she picked up her bag and breezed in. Ivy and I took three steps back to accommodate her. She was a large figure as wide as she was tall. At least on first sight.

Peeling away layer after layer of clothing, Aunt

Hildegarde reduced, becoming much less rotund and much more angular. Finally, she stood there in woollen trousers and a hairy jumper: a tall, skinny person with short, grey, curly hair on a round head. She reminded me of an upside-down exclamation mark. Within her large woolly boots, as big, wide, and fluffy as Amelia's feet, she'd stored several pairs of shoes and now wore a pair of hand-sewn slippers. I could see the resemblance to Uncle Fitz. Especially the moustache.

"So, what's going on?" Aunt Hildegarde directed the question at me. "And what are you and your little friend doing here? Nothing's happened to your father, has it?"

"No," I said. "He's away. Uncle Fitz is in jail because he's been blamed for the Gremlin going on a ram raid in Grosse Village."

"Really? Hmm. Wouldn't have anything to do with my troublemaking twin, Clive, would it?" Aunt Hildegarde's voice held a steely edge. "Fitz has mentioned in his emails that he's having trouble with him. Clive always was a rotten apple. Fitz has been very upset. It's why I'm visiting now instead of at Christmas. First time home in over thirty years. Didn't he tell you?"

"No." For a moment, suspicion pricked me. But then again, Uncle Fitz hadn't told me about Grosse Village. He took forgetfulness to a whole new level.

"Never mind," Aunt Hildegarde continued. "I'm here now. Soon have Fitz out of clink."

"But he doesn't want that," I said. "That's the problem. Chief Constable Huddle has some stupid plan to catch the thief."

Aunt Hildegarde paused in her gathering up of scattered clothes. "Huddle? I knew him when he was a boy. Don't know how he made Chief Constable. He's less bright than a broken lightbulb. I'll be having words with him."

It occurred to me that Aunt Hildegarde could be useful in battling Huddle. He was more likely to listen to an adult. Especially one who appeared to know his quirks. All I had to do was carefully direct her like a drone.

"Now, where's that housemaid?" Aunt Hildegarde looked around her again. "I'll need her to prepare my room. Oh, what's her name? I forget."

"Glenda," Ivy supplied. "She's in bed suffering from stress."

Aunt Hildegarde raised an eyebrow. "Why am I not surprised?" She sniffed the air. "What's that burning smell?"

"Oh no!" said Ivy, dashing off. "I didn't switch the grill off."

Normally, the smoke alarm would've sounded, but the Gremlin had gnawed it to pieces last week and Uncle Fitz hadn't managed to replace it before his arrest. Aunt Hildegarde opened the front door and gave it several strong swings to waft away the smell of burnt toast.

"Now, Kade. Is there anything else I need to know?"

Before I could answer, an angry buzzing spiked the air. A nippy red sports car screeched to a stop at the bottom of the steps. My heart flipped. At the wheel was Mr Worthington. Darn. What was he doing here? From the radiation emanating out of him, I wasn't sure I wanted to know. Particularly given the scowl he shot me before homing in on Aunt Hildegarde.

"Mr Worthington, Kade's Maths teacher. He forgot his homework. I thought I'd drop it off."

"Lady Withershins, Sir Fitz's sister." Aunt Hildegarde gave his hand a bored shake and then dropped it. "The main gate should be locked," she said to me. "I have a big padlock in my bag. Remind me later, Kade to use it. Padlocks are very useful for keeping out unwanted visitors." She gave Mr Worthington a pointed stare.

Mr Worthington ignored the remark. He peered over Aunt Hildegarde's shoulder into the hallway. "Could I have a word with Sir Fitz? Unfortunately, Kade's grades are slipping." He leaked an oily smile. "I was wondering if Sir Fitz would like me to come up and tutor Kade over the half-term? No charge of course. All part of the Grosse High Student Support Policy."

"Oh, no need," Aunt Hildegarde said, catching a falling sock. "I'm a pretty good mathematician myself. I teach the kiddies from the village near my Himalayan Monastery."

"Lady Hildegarde," Mr Worthington said, all hoity-toity. "With respect, I don't think you can compare *that* kind of schooling with the U.K. National Curric..."

"Recently had two students accepted into Oxford reading Higher Mathematics." Aunt Hildegarde cut him off. She gave me a sly wink. "And Fitz is away on a much deserved break," she added.

Mr Worthington looked like he'd swallowed a wasps' nest. He placed a hand on my shoulder. It was like the cold, bony Touch of Death. "I see. But you won't mind me having a quick word with Kade about his homework?"

Aunt Hildegarde waved a hand, dropping two hats. "Go ahead. Vital stuff, homework."

Suspecting mockery, Mr Worthington's forehead furrowed, but Aunt Hildegarde had her back to him. Tightening his grip on my shoulder he steered me out of earshot.

"Don't think that dear old auntie's arrival changes our little agreement," he muttered.

Mr Worthington didn't know it, but his visit was about to change everything. It meant that I didn't have to wait to get my evidence. I slipped a covert hand into my trouser pocket; my new phone's home... and found that there was no phone there. Or pocket. *Why not?* Stomach tightening, I snatched a glance down at my leg. My heart sank. How stupid was I? Of course, I was still wearing my pyjamas. I glared up at the morning sky. Somebody up there either didn't like me or had a warped sense of humour. Why couldn't things be easy for once?

Unaware, Mr Worthington carried on talking. "Nothing's changed. Anyway, it's obvious that your aunt's as nutty as your uncle." He shoved a piece of paper at me. "This is my contact number. I want a daily report."

I took the note. Caught in his cold, unblinking stare, I could so see Mr Worthington as a crook. But it was strange that he hadn't said a word about Uncle Fitz's holiday being a big fat lie. Perhaps he was faking to try and keep me guessing.

"Kade!" Aunt Hildegarde called from the steps. "Breakfast!"

Mr Worthington gave me a little push. "Go on. Don't keep dear old auntie waiting."

"That's a small piece of Maths," Aunt Hildegarde pointed at the scrap of paper. "Homework was much bigger when I was a girl."

"It's a website address," I lied. "For revision."

Aunt Hildegarde clicked her tongue. "What's wrong with a book? I don't hold with all this technology. Don't even own a basic mobile. I wouldn't have an email address if the monks hadn't set me up with an account on their office laptop. Run along now and have your toast. I'll sort myself out a room." She marched upstairs, leaving a Hansel and Gretel trail of clothing behind her.

I headed for the dining room. Ivy and Joss were sitting at the table. They were making notes on their phones about the best ways to camouflage booby traps.

"Mr Worthington's been," I said, heart pounding again.

Joss leapt up, shoving back his chair. "What? Where is he? We can't miss a golden opportunity to get some dirt on him."

"He's already left." I held up the note. "He's given me his mobile number and wants a daily report."

Me, Myself and I who'd been lying next to the table tried to grab the piece of paper and eat it. I yanked it away. Disappointed, he stole a slice of toast from Joss's plate.

"Oy!" Joss swept his breakfast out of reach. "Greedy mutt!"

Two doggy heads looked away, pretending that nothing had happened, whilst the third slobbered contritely over Joss's shoe.

From the hallway Aunt Hildegarde's voice rose above that of the Gremlin's blowing raspberries. "Gremlin. Stop spraying breadcrumbs or I'll flip you upside down and use you as a hoover."

More raspberries and a screech followed. Calvin wandered in, scratching his head.

"There's a strange old lady out there using the Gremlin as a vacuum cleaner," he said sleepily. "Did you know?"

"That's Aunt Hildegarde, Uncle Fitz's sister," I told him.

"Oh," said Calvin. "Seems she can control the Gremlin."

"Tally ho!" Aunt Hildegarde swept in, rolling the Gremlin upside down in front of her. She had its limbs in one hand and body in the other. The Monster's head trundled along at floor level. "Any crumbs in here?" she asked, making a brisk circuit of the room.

"I'm not sure Uncle Fitz would approve," I said, studying the for once subdued Gremlin. "But that's not to say I don't."

"Fitz is too soft," Aunt Hildegarde sniffed. "This creature needs taking in hand."

I was liking Aunt Hildegarde more and more by the minute. "If we go to the station, Aunt Hildegarde," I said cunningly. "You can tell Uncle Fitz."

"Good idea." Aunt Hildegarde made a neat manoeuvre and vacuumed the Gremlin away, making sure that it didn't miss the corners. Ivy waited until she couldn't be overheard.

"Kade, are you sure she's who she says she is?" she asked. "I mean..."

"That her arrival's a little too convenient and she's strangely competent with ugly mug?" I said. "I know what you mean, but it's not like she's new to the Gremlin's antics." I pointed to a framed photo on the sideboard. It showed Uncle Fitz with bandaged fingers, sitting on a deckchair next to Aunt Hildegarde who had the Gremlin (in its smaller and younger years) imprisoned on her lap. A cot blanket had been wrapped around it as a makeshift straitjacket. The Gremlin glared out malevolently, a knitted baby hat askew on its head. The photo was at least forty years old, but Aunt Hildegarde was easily recognisable.

Ivy remained dubious. "How much have you told her?"

"Nothing," I said. "But don't worry, I've got this.

There's another reason why I suggested going to see Uncle Fitz. He'll know his own sister."

As it was, Aunt Hildegarde's identity was confirmed before that. The blue, flashing light of Huddle's police car, slashed through the dining room window.

Chapter 8

Monsters on Television

"I'm not being pompous, Hildegarde. I have to check every lead when a crime's occurred. It's the *law*." Huddle trembled like a knock-kneed lamb. He stood in the kitchen twisting his cap and bleating at Aunt Hildegarde who wasn't impressed by what she called Huddle's 'complete cheek.'

"I am *not* having my identity and motives questioned by someone I babysat."

"It's my job!" Huddle tried to defend himself, but Aunt Hildegarde wasn't having it.

"Don't you come over all official with me, Eric Huddle. *Your job* indeed. I remember you pilfering apples from our orchard. You weren't so bothered about the law then!"

"I was *eight!*" Huddle protested.

This was so not going well for him. It was clear he wished he'd ignored the anonymous tip off (bet I knew who that was from) that a suspicious visitor had arrived at Grosse Manor.

"And when did it become a crime to come home, eh?" Aunt Hildegarde demanded. "You tell me that? And whilst you're at it, you can also tell me why you're holding Fitz."

(I'd filled her in on Huddle's brainwave.)

"Umm, legalities and all that... stuff." Huddle wilted under Aunt Hildegarde's hostility.

"Rubbish!" Aunt Hildegarde snorted down her long nose. "Charge Fitz or let him go instead of encouraging him to collude with your silly plans."

"Yes, of course. I'll think about it. Have a nice day, Hildegarde." Huddle couldn't get away fast enough. He almost forgot to open the door.

Aunt Hildegarde snorted again. "How dare he question me? He should be out looking for the real culprit and questioning them!"

"It is his job," I said, handing her a mug of coffee. I felt a bit sorry for Huddle. Aunt Hildegarde had shredded him.

"I suppose so," Aunt Hildegarde admitted grudgingly. "But he shouldn't be holding Fitz. Who," she added, "shouldn't be sitting on his bum expecting others to sort things out."

"You tell him that when we see him" I said.

An hour later, Victor drove us all to the village. Delighted at Aunt Hildegarde's return, he increased his driving speed to twenty miles an hour. Glenda, having been forced out of bed and made to resume her duties, had been less pleased.

"It'll stop you moping." Aunt Hildegarde had ignored Glenda's protests that Banshees were supposed to mope. "You're paid to work not wail, so get to it."

We'd left Glenda making half-hearted attempts to dust the staircase, griping about how badly she was being treated. But her attitude was nothing next to Huddle's when Aunt Hildegarde swept in, demanding to see her brother. Uncle Fitz on the other hand was ecstatic. He lit up like a lighthouse on full beam.

"Hildegarde!" he said as his sister bustled into the kitchen where he was washing up. She'd barged straight through the station, ignoring Huddle's protests that all visitors must sign in. Drying his hands on a tea towel, Uncle Fitz grabbed hold of her and slapped enthusiastic kisses on her cheeks. "Dear old thing. Eric said you were here."

"I guess she is who she claims to be," Calvin whispered to me. "I don't think your uncle would hug her like that if she wasn't the real thing."

"I wasn't expecting you." Beaming, Uncle Fitz dragged out a chair from under the kitchen table for his sister.

"Thought you could do with some support," Aunt Hildegarde said. "And clearly I was correct." This last bit was directed at Huddle.

"Now, now, don't blame Eric." Uncle Fitz intervened, sensing antagonism. "I'm not a prisoner; I'm helping him." He tapped the side of his nose knowingly. "We have a plan."

"Yes, a stupid one," I said. "Aunt Hildegarde's come to tell you so."

Uncle Fitz was saved from hearing his sister's

thoughts by Ivy galloping in. She'd been distracted on route by the new extra-large TV that Joe was setting up in the sitting room. I grabbed her before she careered through the wall.

"You've *got* to see what was on last night's *'Is it Real? You Tell Me?'* episode." Ivy gabbled away at a thousand miles per hour. "Come on!" With one hand she plucked at me whilst shoving her brothers in line at the same time. "Hurry. I've got Joe to put it on pause."

In the sitting room, the new TV held a frozen image of the *Is it Real* presenter, Angel LeBlanc, perched on top of a tombstone in the middle of a fake cemetery.

"Press play," Ivy commanded Joe, who did as he was told.

Angel LeBlanc thawed. Her trans-Atlantic drawl filled the room. *"... and that puts an end to last week's Selkie investigation. So, is it true? No, it's not. In future, Mr Johnson, don't drop your old wigs in the sea just because you've had a hair transplant. Now, onto something new. Viewers, let me introduce you to the hot topic of next week's show..."*

A crash of creepy music followed. Angel gave a piranha toothed smile. On the screen behind her blown up to ten times its original size and in its full hairy horribleness flashed a picture of... **the Gremlin.** I wasn't sure if the **DAH, DAH, DAH** came from the T.V. or my imagination. I had to steady myself on the back of an armchair. Angel started talking again.

"We've discovered that the remote, ramshackle village of Grosse, entombed within the haunting Cornish countryside, has fallen prey to a spate of beastly break-ins. But that's not all. No. It Grosse Village also houses its very own Monster Mansion full of creepy critter criminals! The

villager who brought us the story says it's like living in Transylvania. Nights are haunted by bats, boogie monsters and a whole horde of other motley creatures straight out of a horror film..."

Uncle Fitz grabbed the remote and jabbed the pause button. "Who?" he said, ogling the screen. "Who in Grosse Village would betray us like this? Eric, we must find out." Another thought dawned. He pressed his lips together. "What does she mean by 'motley monsters'?"

"Let's see if she says," I said, taking the remote from him. Angel's voice resumed...

"... These creatures have a liking for crime almost as much as they do for terrorising. Our source tells us that, during a break-in on their property, they were confronted by what they describe as a vicious, fanged creature akin to a hairy octopus or giant spider of incredible strength. (There was a dramatic close-up of the Gremlin.) In the struggle that followed, the creature engaged in a tug of war over a camera before making off with it..."

I felt my scalp prickle. Was this 'villager' Mr Worthington up to his sly tricks? My mind buzzed and whirled but finally decided no. If Mr Worthington had known about the burglaries, he'd have said so. Clive then? According to Uncle Fitz, he'd stoop to any level. Then again, wouldn't going public make it harder for him to steal the Monsters?

Angel ended the show with a rousing announcement.

"... So, in true 'Is It Real You Tell Me?' style, and the name of public safety, I'll be visiting Grosse Village with my intrepid camera team in search of this crazy creature and its creepy companions. For the truth, tune in next week at nine. Goodnight viewers, sleep tight and don't let the giant bedbugs bite."

"What are we going to do? What are we going to do?

What are we..." Panicked, Uncle Fitz became stuck in repetition.

Aunt Hildegarde switched off the T.V. "Calm down, Fitz," she said.

But Uncle Fitz carried on panicking. His eyebrows and moustache twitched faster than the Hadron Collider. "But if they discover the Monsters..."

"We'll make sure they don't," I interrupted, experiencing further twinges of guilt at Uncle Fitz's distress. This was all my fault. Why hadn't I taken better care of my phone in the first place? I swore to myself that I'd make it up to Uncle Fitz.

"We'll hide the Monsters," I said. "If Angel LeBlanc can't find them, she won't stay. The problem is *where* do we put them? We can't use the village if Angel's heading there."

Ivy gave me a pity smile. "Rubbish plan then, eh? What else have you got?"

I was about to say that I was open to suggestions when my mobile rang. *Unknown Caller* flashed up on the screen. Without thinking, I pressed the answer button.

"Jones! What the HELL is going on?" Mr Worthington's rabid voice slammed into my ears, clanging against my eardrums. Hands shaking like mixer on full speed I almost lost my grip on the phone. Why hadn't I changed my number. I guessed that Mr Worthington had withheld his in case I'd not answered.

"Who is it?" Calvin asked, puzzled. When I mouthed *Mr Worthington*, he almost fell over. Aunt Hildegarde and Huddle looked puzzled.

"Hold on, I'm putting it on speaker," I said in a low voice. "Everyone, stay quiet."

"How has the presenter of that stupid show got hold

of a picture of the Gremlin?" Mr Worthington thundered. "What do they know in Grosse Village?"

I could dismiss him as the 'villager'. He was in a right mood.

"I don't know," I said to both questions. "Don't blame me. It's not my fault that someone rang the show. You can't expect me to control what the villagers do. I'm not..."

"Why didn't you tell me about the Gremlin re-enacting a Viking rampage?" Mr Worthington's angry interruption railroaded through my sentence.

"I couldn't; I lost your number," I lied. Ivy gave me a thumbs up for quick thinking.

A long pause followed whilst Mr Worthington decided whether to believe me or not.

Eventually, his voice as tight as a stretched elastic band, he said, "We need to talk. I'm coming over."

Joss scribbled something on his hand, which he stuck in front of me.

"You can't," I said, reading his palm. "My aunt's organised a get to know each other day, because..."

Calvin wrote furiously on his twin's other hand.

"... we don't know each other," I finished.

"And how long is this going to take?" Mr Worthington's mood wasn't improving.

"Umm, today and tomorrow." Having run out of script I improvised. "And I won't be able to phone because she says I'm not to use any gadgets. She doesn't approve of them."

"And where, pray, are you going?" Mr Worthington enquired in a tone that you could have chipped ice off.

Joss scribbled something on Ivy's hand and held it up.

"Dunno," I read out. "It's a mystery trip."

Another long silence. Then, Mr Worthington snarled, "I'll be round in the morning at nine o'clock sharp, the day after tomorrow. Be there." He closed the call.

We all looked at each other.

"I guess that's bought us some time," I said. "But not much."

"I apologise, Kade," Uncle Fitz said, looking stunned. "There's something seriously wrong with your teacher. I shall write to the school governors."

"Yeah, I told you that," I said. "Now do you believe that he's in with Clive?"

"What's he got to do with Clive?" Aunt Hildegarde immediately asked. I told her.

Aunt Hildegarde listened, mulled it all over and then said, "From what I've heard, Fitz, I'd say that Kade's on the ball about our brother and this schoolteacher chappie being a team.

Probably was him whom that Troll saw skedaddling. Besides, Clive's always had others doing his dirty work in case it goes wrong."

"I'd better go and arrest them," Huddle said, straightening the buttons on his uniform.

"How?" I asked, "when you don't know where they are?"

"Umm, good point." Huddle drooped at having an arrest snatched away from him.

"The first and most important thing to do now," Uncle Fitz said, "is to move theMonsters. Kade's spot on. They need to be hidden away from this Angel woman."

"How about we ship them off to my Himalayan monastery?" Aunt Hildegarde said.

"Won't the monks mind?" Ivy asked. "I would."

"Yeah," I said. "Don't you go to monasteries to get away from chaos, not invite it in?"

"Oh, they're an enlightened lot, nothing fazes them,"

Aunt Hildegarde replied. "Life there will be good for the Monsters, the monks will teach them how to meditate. And that Banshee how to clean properly," she added. "They're very particular."

"But how do we get them to Nepal?" Calvin said. "It's not down the road. How do you book airplane tickets for Monsters? What about quarantine regulations, visas; all that stuff?"

"Oh, I don't think we need to bother with those little matters. I never have." Uncle Fitz chirped up, happier now that something concrete was being done.

"Exactly," Aunt Hildegarde agreed. "Overthinking complicates things. The Monsters can leave in the same way that I arrived. A special boat on undercover manoeuvres."

"You came here undercover?" I gaped. Wow. Aunt Hildegarde was an international woman of mystery. "Wicked. Do you work for MI5 or something?"

"No," I hitched a lift. I'd spent the last of the savings from selling my hand knitted llama wool socks on getting to the port. It was the crew who were operating undercover. For security. Their ways are a little unorthodox. Anyway, they're a non-profit group called OPSA: Organisation for the Preservation of Strange Animals. If they hear of any strange creature in trouble, they rescue and re-home it in a safe environment."

"In that case, perhaps they can find a deserted tropical island for Amelia because she'll have a real hissy fit if you stick her back in the Himalayas," I said.

"Good point, Kade." Uncle Fitz's worried frown came back. "Amelia's very delicate."

"Hmm." Aunt Hildegarde had a quick re-think. "Maybe the monastery's not the best place. I'll call OPSA. I'm sure they'll know of a lovely location for each

Monster. It's best if you talk to them too, Fitz. We'll call them once we're back at the manor."

"I can't come back to the manor. Not as things stand," Uncle Fitz said. "No, no. That won't do at all. If Clive were to see me, he'd realise there's something fishy going on."

"How? He obviously doesn't know you've been arrested," I said. "Or Mr Worthington would have tried to use it against me."

But Uncle Fitz was adamant. "They could be pretending. Can't take the risk." He patted his sister's hand. "It won't matter if Clive sees you, Hildegarde. He'll simply think that you've come to visit. He won't think there's anything strange in that."

"After thirty years?" I said. "Really? You don't think he'll be suspicious by her sudden arrival? I was and I'm family. That's why I brought her here, so you could check her out."

"Thanks very much," Aunt Hildegarde said, in a vinegary tone. "It's nice to know I have such trusting relatives."

But Uncle Fitz wouldn't be persuaded. Huddle of course backed him up. (He wasn't giving up on his stupid plan of waiting instead of doing.)

Finally accepting defeat, Aunt Hildegarde drew herself up to her full height. Towering over her brother, she said crossly, "Fitz, all the stress you've been under has scrambled your brain. I'm going now. I shall call you later when you'll hopefully be more reasonable. Come along, children." She swept out.

Uncle Fitz gawked after her, his mouth opening and closing silently. He tried appealing to me, but I was on Aunt Hildegarde's side. "You should listen to her, " I told him.

Back at the Manor, Aunt Hildegarde refused to let us boobytrap the grounds.

"You could seriously hurt somebody," she said. "It's illegal."

"It's illegal to smuggle the Monsters out of the country but that doesn't bother you!" I argued. We'd shown her the gadgets thinking she'd be all for it, but she wasn't.

"The padlock will keep people out," she said, standing her ground.

"That didn't work with Mr Worthington," I said. "He came over the wall."

Ivy, who'd been looking out of the window added to the discussion. "If anyone cares, I can see a T.V. Studio van coming up the drive."

"What?" Aunt Hildegarde zoomed to the window. "They must have picked the lock! I'll have them up for breaking and entering."

We rushed over to the window. Rumbling towards the house was a big, yellow RV with the words: *Is It Real? You Tell Me!* stencilled on the sides in electric blue. A man jumped down from the front followed by another carrying a holdall. The first man jogged round to the back of the vehicle, opened the doors and helped out Angel LeBlanc. In real life, she presented as even more intimidating figure than on telly. The type who's tricky to get rid of. Angel didn't waste any time. She strode up to the front door and yanked on the bell, which clanged out a series of loud, furious chimes in protest.

"Enemy at twelve o'clock!" Ivy yelled. "***DUCK***!" She dived behind the sofa.

Not having met with any success at the door, Angel

and her team peered through the windows. We copied Ivy and hid behind the nearest pieces of furniture as the presenter rapped on the glass. Eventually she got bored and went away, but not before shoving something through the letterbox. There was a metallic **THUD** as the cover fell back in place. Seconds later we heard the R.V.'s engine roar into life. Even so, we stayed hidden for a few minutes more. Then we charged to the front door. Ivy got there first. She picked up a piece of paper. It had a business card attached to it. Ivy read it out loud.

"Angel LeBlanc: T.V. Personality, Presenter and Reporter," she paused. "She wants an interview about the Monsters. She says the studios are happy to pay for any meetings."

"How much?" I asked.

Ivy gawked at me. "Are you serious?"

I gave her head a pity pat. "Duh! Not in the way you're thinking. But once the Monsters are safe, we could charge Angel lots of dosh to come in, at which point she'll find nothing and go away whilst we keep the money. The end."

"Sounds good to me," said Joss.

"Yes, you get to meet Angel," Calvin added, flashing Joss a wicked grin. Joss hit him.

"I'll get on with contacting OPSA." Aunt Hildegarde separated the two brothers.

"And I'll speak to Uncle Fitz and warn him about Angel in case she comes to the station," I said. "Plus the Monsters need checking on."

"Good thinking," Aunt Hildegarde said approvingly. "We'll meet back here in an hour."

I checked the time. "Okay, but we don't say anything to the Monsters. The Gremlin will cause trouble and Amelia's not good with change."

"OPSA are happy to help," Aunt Hildegarde announced an hour later.

This was good. Unfortunately, it didn't solve the problem of how to get the Monsters to safety without ending up on national television. Angel and her crew had disappeared from the grounds, but they'd now set up camp on the other side of the gates. I phoned Huddle. Not that he was of any help.

"I can't do anything," he said. "They're outside the grounds so they're not trespassing. Unless they're doing something illegal, they can stand where they like."

"But they broke in earlier," I objected. "I sent you a picture of the padlock."

"Which remains locked in position on the gate," Huddle replied. "And I rang Miss Le Blanc on the number you gave me. She said she doesn't know what you're talking about."

"What else would she say?" I snapped. Honestly. What was wrong with Huddle?

"It's your word against hers. I can't arrest her just because you want me to," Huddle said. "Get in touch if she starts being a nuisance but until then, don't."

Fortunately, Uncle Fitz was ex-directory so Angel couldn't pester us with phone calls. However, she remained stubbornly standing at the gates.

"That must count as being a nuisance," Aunt Hildegarde said. "I'll call Huddle again."

But the next minute, Angel and her team jumped into their RV and drove off.

"Perhaps they've got bored and gone home," Ivy suggested. I didn't think so. Angel didn't strike me as the giving up type.

"I bet she's driven to the village to talk to her source." I said.

Calvin folded his arms. "Whoever they are won't be popular when the rest of the villagers get their hands on them. They're going to need a good disguise."

"That's it!" I punched Calvin's shoulder. "You've given me a great idea for how to get rid of Angel. Disguise," I explained as everyone looked at me, baffled.

Calvin rubbed his shoulder. "What's that got to do with hitting me?"

"Nothing," I said. "I'm talking about fooling Angel. We'll make mock-ups of some of the Monsters – and of you, Aunt Hildegarde so that it looks like they have a guard – stick them in the car and get Victor to drive off on a wild goose chase."

"And Angel LeBlanc will race off after him. **YES!**" Aunt Hildegarde punched the air.

"Then," I finished, "we can move the Monsters without her snooping. "By the time she realises she's been tricked, it'll be too late."

Joss and Calvin each gave me a high-five.

"Brilliant," Joss said. "Let's get moving!"

We rushed off to collect anything we could use for what we codenamed Operation Monster Load.

Chapter 9

Operation Overload

I vy and Joss set up a model-making studio in the library – they were the best at D.T. The job was demanding. And smelly. The jumbled aromas of glue, paint and the fusty, old clothes gathered from long unopened wardrobes didn't mix. Until Ivy lit some scented candles, we all had to keep sticking our heads out of the window for gulps of fresh air.

"Something Yeti coloured." Aunt Hildegarde handed me the white, fluffy coat she'd arrived in, flinching as the clangs of a metallic sounding avalanche jangled in from the hallway. "Oh dear!" She rushed out. I followed. Calvin had knocked an Amelia sized suit of armour down the staircase. On its journey, it had split into a zillion bits.

"Calvin!" Aunt Hildegarde threw up her hands in exasperation. "With a bit of work, that suit could have passed for Amelia. Now all it could pass for is a jigsaw puzzle."

"Not my fault!" Calvin, red cheeked and panting, tumbled down the stairs almost as fast as the armour had. "I was running for my life. See?" He tugged at the neck of his sweatshirt, which looked like it had been used in a tug of war. "An elephant could wear this. Mum's going to go mental! It's that Gremlin. It's learnt how to pick locks. I caught it slithering down the landing and when I tried to stop it, it went for me. It should be charged with GBH."

Aunt Hildegarde's jaw tightened. Striding over to the umbrella stand she selected a lethal looking brolly. "I refuse to put up with that creature's nonsense anymore. Where is it?"

"On the second floor, mangling whatever it can get its fangs into," Calvin said.

"I. Shall. Be. Back. In. A. Few. Minutes." Aunt Hildegarde marched upstairs; each word punctuated by an echoing stamp.

I picked up the fallen helmet from the suit of armour. Its large, scarlet feather drooped; another victim of the Gremlin.

I looked at Calvin. "Do you think we should offer to help?"

"Probably," Calvin replied, as Me, Myself and I gambolled up. "But let's go with no."

Meanwhile, the dog had fallen in love with the metal helmet. **SLAP!** A colossal paw swiped the headpiece out of my hands. Me, Myself and I dived after it, his heads fighting for the feather. The middle head won. Tearing the plume free he scampered off into the library.

"Oh, let him have it," I said. "It'll keep him out of trouble." There was a loud crash followed by a yelp. "Or not," I added as Joss's angry voice demanded to know who'd given that 'stupid mutt' that 'stupid feather'.

We went to investigate. The library gave the

impression that a tank had ploughed through. Several models lay in pieces, courtesy of a howling, giant dog. Having accidentally knocked over the candles, he'd set the feather on fire and was now zooming around the rug in terrified circles. I whipped a vase from the mantlepiece, chucked away the flowers and threw the water over him. We all told off Me, Myself and I whose response was to eat the feather.

"What's happened here?" Aunt Hildegarde strode in carrying the umbrella, now bent out of shape and in tatters. "Who's the pyromaniac?" She pointed at the ruined rug.

"The dog," I said. "What happened to the umbrella?"

"Sacrificed in the line of duty," Aunt Hildegarde replied. "But the Gremlin's padlocked in the second-floor closet. I strongly recommend that none of you go near it until OPSA arrive."

"No worries," Calvin said with feeling, fingering his ruined sweatshirt.

Aunt Hildegarde had arranged for OPSA to arrive once Angel was safely off chasing Victor. By coincidence they were in Cornwall, responding to a reported unicorn sighting. Or, as they'd explained to Aunt Hildegarde, what they'd thought was a unicorn.

"Turned out to be an old billy goat with one horn," Aunt Hildegarde told us. "And very nasty tempered too. Chased a team member up a tree and the rest into their van. The poor dears were stuck there for hours, whilst the goat lurked below, giving them the evil eye."

"Why didn't they use tranquiliser guns?" I asked.

Aunt Hildegarde gave a low, sorry whistle. "The one in the tree forgot to pack them. It was his first day. Barb; OPSA's C.E.O, isn't sure he's cut out for the job. But it all worked out when the goat got bored and wandered off. They'll be here late tomorrow morning."

"How are they going to control the Monsters if they can't deal with a goat?" I asked.

Aunt Hildegarde brushed this aside. "That was the newbie's fault. The rest of the group are very experienced."

I hoped so. Still, once the models were revamped, they looked brilliant. Especially the mock-up of Amelia. It was dressed in Aunt Hildegarde's coat hung over a second suit of armour (Calvin had found a spare at the back of the attic), and a very realistic Yeti mask made by Ivy. Pleased with the results, we decided that the time had arrived for the next part of our strategy. Briefing Victor.

I rang him and explained the plan. "Be here at seven a.m. tomorrow," I said, once he'd grasped the plot. "And don't forget the spare padlock key that we gave you. Make a big show of being up to something when you open the gates... Yes, Angel will follow you. That's the point! We want her to think we're up to something. Be particularly shifty when you drive into the garage... No, not *that* kind of driving into it! I mean open the *door* and drive in. And close it after you so that we can load up without an audience."

Victor arrived the next morning, making a big, noisy pantomime out of opening the gates to attract Angel. He did. Especially when he almost ran over her cameraman.

"If he stands in the middle of the road then what does he expect?" Victor snapped.

"Actually, he was standing on the grass," Ivy replied. She'd been hiding in the bushes at the time, keeping tabs on Angel and her team. "When did you last have an eye test?"

Victor glared at her.

Sensing war, I bundled Ivy out of the room. "Let's get going."

Victor was amazed by our creativity. He moved from model to model as though they were prized exhibits at the Tate Modern.

"Oh my," he said, tapping the shoulder of a scarecrow with a spiky wig and a pair of yellow false teeth stuck in its pumpkin head. "Ingenious. This one's the spitting image of you, Lady Hildegarde."

Aunt Hildegarde gave him a frosty look. "That one is supposed to be a Troll." Picking up the Yeti decoy, she stomped off towards the little storeroom at the back of the house that led into the garage.

Finally, we had all the decoys arranged snugly in the car. As a finishing touch, I trapped the tail of a large toy dog in the boot.

"Something else to tempt Angel with. Uncle Fitz's Hound of Doom."

"But your uncle doesn't have a Hound of Doom," Ivy said.

"No, but Angel doesn't know that," I replied. "And if an idea presents then use it!"

As I spoke, Glenda presented herself and marched up to the car, a large carpetbag clutched in one hand. She was wearing her best coat. On top of her veil, which she'd thrown forwards to hide her Banshee features, perched a wide brimmed hat.

"I'm going with Victor," Glenda announced,

sweeping away the model from the front seat. She settled herself in its place. "I don't like boats. I get seasick. I'm off to stay with a cousin in Blackpool. Victor can drop me at the bus station."

Aunt Hildegarde shrugged. "Whatever. We don't have time to argue." She pushed the model aside with her foot. "Back into the house everyone in case Miss Nosey is lurking about."

I knocked on Victor's window. He wound down the glass and thrust out his crabby face.

"Time to roll, Victor," I said.

Victor pressed his remote fob and slid the car into gear as the garage door lifted. We all retreated through the entrance leading back inside the house. A couple of minutes later my phone rang. I put it on speaker.

"All clear." Victor's voice grated out. "I'm approaching the gates."

The car had a hands-free system and Victor had instructions to stay in touch. He droned on, giving boring and unnecessary details of every rock, stick and blade of grass he passed.

I shoved my phone at Ivy. "Here, you said you'd like to try it out."

Ivy put her hands behind her back. "I've changed my mind."

"What happened to teamwork?" I challenged. "We need to know where Victor is."

"Oh, give it here, I'll do it," Aunt Hildegarde took the phone from me. "But this means that you'll have to get the Monsters ready for the move without me."

"Fair enough," Calvin said, eying the mobile like it was the Kiss of Death.

At that moment, the landline rang. It was OPSA calling to say they were making great time and would be here early. However, they were down a pair of hands; their newest recruit had snuck away in the night, leaving behind a note saying they'd decided on a career change.

"Okay, guys," I said. "Time to get going on the real Operation Monster Load."

Question: How do you get a bunch of un-cooperative Monsters into a van?

Answer: With the greatest of difficulty.

We went off in pairs to inform the Monsters about the upcoming move and get them ready. Me with Joss and Ivy with Calvin. The problem was the Monsters didn't want to leave.

The Trolls expressed this in very blunt terms.

"Bog off! Yer Uncle's not said nowt about it so get lost," one of them growled, flashing me a rude sign with his fingers, before kicking Joss on the shins. When we didn't leave quickly enough, we were tied up in toilet paper and dumped outside the bathroom door.

"You know what?" Joss said, unwinding himself. "I've changed my mind. I'd rather be bored to death by Victor than explain to the Trolls why they're being evicted."

"Let's give them some time to get used to the idea and then try again," I suggested.

But the Trolls weren't having it. Every time we tried talking to them, they flushed themselves down the loo. We sent Ivy in as a scare tactic to force the Trolls into surrender, but this had them moving twice as fast.

"Oh no, it's that girl again!" they yelled, knocking seconds off their flushing speed.

In the end, I decided that we'd have to resort to

trickery and came up with a cunning plan. First, I got Joss to help me knock over and empty a large rainwater barrel from the garden. Next, I removed the cover from the drain that the Trolls used as an exit. Step three was to send Ivy back inside the bathroom. As expected, the Trolls leapt down the u-bend the second they saw her. But this time, we were ready. Armed with Uncle Fitz's long-handled butterfly nets, designed to catch the giant variety, (obviously) we netted them as they helter-skeltered down the loo and popped out of the drain before dumping them into the barrel. Once we had them all, we slammed on the lid. I sat on top of it whilst Joss hammered it in place.

"Hurry," I gasped as the barrel bucked under me, its furious contents screeching threats. "OWWW!" A hairy hand sneaked out from a gap and pinched me hard on the thigh. "Naughty Troll!" Joss hit the Troll's fingers with the hammer.

Meanwhile, Calvin and Ivy played hide and seek with the Shapeshifter who'd very cunningly hidden itself but was eventually discovered disguised as a wall stain. Luckily, it fell in love with its stress-free travelling arrangements – an empty, plain, wooden box – and from then on behaved.

Amelia wasn't so easily convinced. Nervous by nature, having a house move thrown at her put her in meltdown. She huddled howling in a heavy heap at the back of her sauna, her large, hairy arms folded tight and refused to budge.

"Come on, Amelia," I cajoled, checking my watch; we were running out of time. Angel could realise at any moment that she'd been fooled. She might already be on her way back. "It's for your own good. Honest."

Amelia howled even louder.

"Oh come *on*," I said, exasperated. "We're trying to *save* you!"

Screwing up her mouth, the Yeti burst into angry tears. All further attempts to persuade were met with seething silence. I left her with Joss and returned with a jug of cold water.

"You leave me no choice," I said, dousing the coals. "No more sauna."

Amelia flinched. Sticking on a bobble hat in response to the slightly lowered temperature she yowled pitifully but still wouldn't shift.

"You're next," I said, brandishing the jug. "I hate using force but you're not giving me any choice."

The Yeti pouted and covered her head with a thermal blanket.

"Fine," I said, handing the jug to Joss. "Refill, please."

At this a horrified Amelia swept the blanket away. I raised an eyebrow. Even given the whiteness of her fur, the Yeti visibly paled. Next second, she shot howling out of the door, pausing en route to grab several scarves. However, once she saw how cosy we'd made her crate with duvets, thermal blankets, battery heated cushions and hot water bottles dressed in teddy bear covers she cheered up and shuffled inside where she curled up, purring.

"That's the register completed." Ivy ticked names off on her phone's clipboard. "Apart from Old Smokey, the Gremlin, and the dog." A heavy thumping from above almost caused an accidental deleting of the list. Ivy gave the ceiling a fierce scowl. "I wish the Gremlin would shut up."

The booming thuds, crashes and murderous screams coming from the imprisoned Gremlin were horrendous. The Monster had learnt of the move through the keyhole and had gone bananas: very hypocritical seeing that it'd caused all the trouble in the first place. Old Smokey was equally anti-social, huffing and puffing so much that it was impossible to get close without risking death by frying.

"Forget it," I said, ducking a blast of fire. "He can be OPSA's problem."

"So that leaves Me, Myself and I," Calvin said, sucking a red burn on his wrist.

"No worries." I patted two of the dog's heads whilst the third nibbled my shoelaces. "Chuck a couple of bones into his crate and he'll be no trouble."

My plan worked. The inclusion of three large, meaty bones, arranged in the crate on a bed of biscuits, had the dog's noses twitching straightaway. Me, Myself and I made feverish little noises of longing.

"Off you go, then," I said. "Into the crate."

The dog was inside in seconds. He lay down snuffling happily, jaws locked around his tasty reward whilst we shut him in. Of course, because this had been so easy, a problem had to follow. The doorbell rang.

"Blimey," said Calvin. "Is that OPSA? That was quick."

"Someone answer the door!" bawled Aunt Hildegarde from upstairs where she was hunting for Amelia's favourite cuddly toy.

"I'll go," Calvin said, padding out of the room. A few seconds later we heard the door creak open and then slam shut.

"Help!" Calvin's voice screeched out. "It's Mr Worthington!"

I leapt up from locking the dog's crate. *Mr Worthington?*

"*What?* Are you sure?" I felt my heart launch itself

into a five-k run.

There was the sound of the door rasping open again.

"Yes, absolutely sure! *Oh no..!*" Sounds of ferocious scuffling followed.

Mr Worthington's voice filled the distance between us. **"KADE JONES! I KNOW YOU'RE THERE! COME OUT NOW!"**

The ferocious tone made my heart hammer even more. Joss grabbed his sister and shoved her behind him.

"**JONES!**" Mr Worthington bellowed again.

"He's not here," I heard Calvin lie. "Ow! Let go of my ear!"

"Don't lie, Simpkins, whichever one you are," Mr Worthington snarled. "I saw that car leave and at the slow speed it was going, I'd have to be blind not to realise Jones wasn't in it!"

"OWW!" Calvin howled again.

At this second shriek, Joss launched himself out of the door. "Leave my brother alone!" he yelled, rushing off in defence of his twin. I moved to follow but Ivy grabbed my arm.

"Don't," she said. "It's you Mr Worthington wants."

"OUCH! Mind the stud!"

Mr Worthington must have Joss by the ear too. Ivy growled from deep in her throat, her nose wrinkled up like an angry miniature bulldog.

"Nobody touches my brothers apart from me." She released my arm. "Don't worry, bros, I'm coming!" she yelled, flying off with me in close pursuit.

Mr Worthington, holding the twins by the ear, gave a nasty grin when he saw me. He licked his thin lips. "Now we're all here you can tell me what's going on."

Nobody said anything. Mr Worthington looked at

each of us in turn, his face like granite.

"Like it or not, you *will* cooperate," he said in response to the silence. "You're a moron, Jones if you didn't think I'd check up on you. Family get-together my foot. I know your uncle's in jail."

"And I know you're his crooked brother's minion!" I slapped back, meeting his glare. "And you should both be in jail – one for the criminally deranged!"

"Clive Withershins' minion? Me?" Mr Worthington blustered and gobbled like an outraged turkey. "Don't insult me, you idiot boy. Now let me in. We've important things to discuss." He gave the door a hard shove with his shoulder, catapulting the twins headfirst into the umbrella stand. "Jones, where has your aunt taken the Monsters?"

At least the models had fooled him.

"Somewhere you'll never know," Calvin panted, wrenching his twin free.

"*What?*" Mr Worthington morphed into a human Gremlin, smashing through the hallway like a howling tornado. Petrified, the twins barricaded themselves behind a large golfing umbrella. I dragged Ivy to the shelter offered at the back of a human-sized Ming vase. Mr Worthington continued banging on the wooden panelling, kicking the skirting boards and cursing. Mostly at us.

"What have you *done?*" His screeching peppered the air. "You interfering *brats!*"

"We are all so failing Maths this year," I mouthed at Calvin and Joss.

"Do you know what those Monsters are *worth?*" Mr Worthington continued raging. "Do you know what people would *pay* for them? Do you know what they can *do* with them?" By now, his complexion had changed from pink, to red, to an interesting shade of purple.

"I know that we've outsmarted you," I said, with more bravado than I felt.

Mr Worthington roared like a category five hurricane and grabbed a walking stick from the stand. Shoving the twins golfing umbrella out of his way he leapt at me. *SWISH*. Despite my best efforts to dodge, the stick caught me neatly across the backside. I yelped as a fiery pain seared my rear end.

"Enemy fire at one o'clock!" Ivy yelled, out-manoeuvring Mr Worthington's efforts to also introduce her to the stick.

"Oy, pick on somebody your own size!" Calvin and Joss flung themselves at Mr Worthington. He stumbled, giving Ivy time to skip the next strike.

"Hey!" I yelled, attempting to distract him. "Over here!"

"I'll get your auntie, Kade." Ivy pelted up the stairs as Aunt Hildegarde flew down. Where'd she been? How could she not have heard all the commotion?

"Why were you so long?" Ivy demanded. "Didn't you hear all the noise?"

"The Gremlin stuck a tentacle under the closet door and grabbed my ankle. Took me forever to free myself," Aunt Hildegarde panted. "What's going on? Why is Worthington here? No, Kade, not *THAT* picture, it's priceless!"

Too late. I'd already smacked Mr Worthington over the head with it. Aunt Hildegarde winced as the gilded frame splintered. She winced a second time as the man stumbled about in a confused daze, wearing the painting like an Elizabethan ruff. Groaning, he bumped into the side of the huge, antique chest that Uncle Fitz kept in the hallway.

Seeing a temporary solution to the problem I nudged

Ivy, indicating the enormous trunk with my head. Ivy nodded. On the count of a silently mouthed *one... two... three,* we nipped forward and heaved open its heavy lid. As Mr Worthington rolled past for a second time, Ivy rolled herself in front of his feet. Tumbling over her he smacked into the wall, bounced off and teetered this way and that, moaning pathetically. As he staggered in my direction, I thrust out a leg, neatly tripping him up. Mr Worthington, toppled forwards, backwards, sideways and finally finished up inside the chest. It swallowed him in a single greedy gulp. ***BANG!*** A corner of the lid splintered as it slammed shut. I slid the thick, metal bolts across, locking Mr Worthington inside.

"I say, Kade," Aunt Hildegarde protested. "First the painting and now Great Uncle Nathaniel's oak seafaring trunk. Please be more careful with the family heirlooms."

Inside the chest, Mr Worthington battered angrily at the lid. Aunt Hildegarde bent down and slid back the bolts. She raised the lid slightly. The muffled rant, "Listen... don't understand... Clive... important deal!" clawed their way out.

Aunt Hildegarde let the lid slam back in place. "Well," she said. "Clearly he *has* got something going on with my brother."

"Should we hand him over to Huddle?" I asked her.

"No, Huddle's a duffer. There's a good chance he'll let Worthington escape whilst making a cup of tea," Aunt Hildegarde replied. "I've a better idea. We'll send him off with the Monsters. OPSA can unload him somewhere far away. Somewhere it'll be difficult for him to get back from."

And bang on cue, OPSA arrived.

Chapter 10

Taken for a Ride

O PSA drove up in two huge, logoed trucks, large enough to house London Zoo. They'd also brought a reinforced iron cage for the Gremlin.

"That was my idea," Aunt Hildegarde said. "Health and Safety precautions. Don't want them suing us if the thing breaks out and causes a traffic accident."

"Nothing could break out of this," said the big, square shouldered man dressed in biker leather and steampunk goggles who was unloading the cage. "Isn't that true, Barb?"

"Absolutely, Bonzo." A tall woman wearing a t-shirt bearing the logo **'WEIRD IS WONDERFUL'** followed the cage down the ramp. She gave Aunt Hildegarde a cheery wave. "Hello, Lady Withershins, nice to see you again."

From the cab of the second truck, another man and woman appeared.

"Phil and Suze," Aunt Hildegarde said, pointing at them. "Barb, this is my nephew, Kade; and his friends Calvin, Joss and Ivy."

"Hi," Barb said. "Now, where are all these lovely animals in need of a safe, new home?"

"Snugly wrapped up and ready to go," Aunt Hildegarde replied. "Excluding the Gremlin and Dragon. We can't get near them."

Barb flashed a confident smile. "No problem. We can deal with anything."

"How about goats?" I murmured. Then louder, "Have you brought the tranquiliser guns?"

Ten minutes later, the OPSA team stood in the courtyard, half-comatose with shock. Bonzo couldn't stop shaking. If Suze and Barb hadn't been holding him up he'd have rattled apart. Phil was crying for his mum. Aunt Hildegarde doused the final smoulders from their tattered clothes with the garden hose. The bits the Gremlin hadn't shredded, Old Smokey had fireballed.

"I think the tranquiliser idea's a good one." Suze examined her melted wristwatch.

Bonzo shook his shaved head. "I resign."

Barb was made of sterner stuff. Either that or self-preservation wasn't high on her list of priorities. "We're here to do a job," she snapped at her team. "I'm getting the necessary equipment from the truck and then we're going back in." She pounded off towards the vehicles.

I tagged along. "I'll help you," I said, jogging alongside. "But I'd suggest a double dose of tranquiliser if you want to get within ten miles of the Gremlin."

At the back of the first truck, a huge metal box as long and deep as a chest freezer, held a whole world of equipment: weighted nets, tranquiliser guns, darts, two-way radios, infrared cameras, locks; and strangely, a mix of musical instruments.

Barb gestured at a second box. "Could you get some extra weighted nets from in there?"

I heaved off the heavy lid. This box was in worse condition. It was old, rusty and had loads of nasty nails sticking up from its edges like a bad-toothed Troll. The nails proved to be as tricky as the Trolls. One sneakily impaled itself through my T-shirt, hanging on with alligator strength. It was like playing tug of war. The more I struggled, the more the nail bit in. Being firmly embedded in the rim, it had the advantage: unlike me, it couldn't lose its balance. The tussle ended with me taking a head dive into the box. The nets rippled beneath the impact. It was like drowning in a mesh sea.

Barb hoisted me out. "We don't have time for playing," she tutted, followed by a sharp, "What's that you're holding?"

Something had resurfaced along with me. A sheet of paper. It must have been inside the box already and I'd grabbed hold of it without realising. I'd about enough time to read the heading with the first letter of each name highlighted, before Barb snatched it away.

O'Neil, Patching, Solomon & Adams Truck Hire: The One Place Stop!

"It's rude to read other people's mail." Barb stepped up so close that I could feel her breath. Her eyes bit into mine. I swear there were flecks of ice bobbing around the pupils. I tried to say that I wasn't being nosey, but her frostiness froze my words.

Barb shoved the sheet of paper into her jeans pocket. Tossing the nets and tranquiliser guns into a rucksack, she hoisted the bag onto her shoulder, blasted me a final Arctic stare and left. I didn't start to defrost until the sound of her footsteps had faded away. Blimey! What was her problem? You'd think I'd been in possession of top-secret data, not boring office work. I was really glad that she'd disappeared behind the other truck. Its huge, slanted OPSA logo glinted in the sun. If it hadn't been for Barb's strange behaviour, I wouldn't have given it a second thought, but the incident had left me tingling with suspicion.

It was the logo.

I frowned. For some reason, the letter order niggled me. I had this weird feeling that I was seeing but at the same time *missing* something. I read the logo again and again trying to figure it out. My mind spun with possibilities, none of them quite fitted. Then **BAM!** Like water surging through a flood barrier the answer swirled in. OPSA wasn't solely an abbreviation for Organisation for the Protection of Strange Animals, it could also be an abbreviation for O'Neil, Patching, Solomon and Adams.

Aunt Hildegarde appeared in reverse order of the route taken by Barb and came clumping up the truck's ramp. "There you are, Kade." She stopped when she saw my expression. "What's wrong?"

"Aunt Hildegarde!" My words spilt out in pure relief that she wasn't Barb. "I'm so glad to see you. I think there's something weird about OPSA. Barb threatened me. I found a piece of paper; some type of document, I think, in there." I pointed to the box. "It was from a truck hire company. Barb snatched it and went all weird." I shivered. "She was dead scary."

A funny look came over Aunt Hildegarde as if she was either thinking really fast or trying not to laugh. "Were the names O'Neil, Patching, Solomon and Adams on the document?"

My head shot up, puzzled. "How did you know?"

"And being a clever boy, you worked out that if you take the first letter of each name you end up with OPSA?"

"Yes."

Aunt Hildegarde chuckled. "O'Neil is Barb's last name. Her mum's a partner in a trucking firm. Barb borrows their trucks. Running a non-profit organisation, she relies on family help but doesn't like people knowing. Creates a bad impression if competitors go about saying you can't support your own company. I think Barb's nerves are a little edgy after what happened with the Gremlin and Old Smokey"

I wasn't convinced. "But don't you find it a bit too... convenient. And even if it's true, why do both organisations have the same name?"

"It's deliberate," Aunt Hildegarde said. "Barb feels it inspires confidence if people think that these expensive trucks are hers. It's called careful marketing."

"Are you sure?" I pressed, not yet convinced. "Don't you find it... odd? I do."

Aunt Hildegarde took this personally. "For one so young you've a very suspicious mind," she said tartly. "I'll have you know that I'm an excellent judge of character."

"But how well do you know *them*?" I said, feeling a need to defend myself.

Aunt Hildegarde wasn't having it. "Enough to know that you're being silly. I don't want to hear another word. Back to the yard. We've Monsters to save." She paraded me back to the courtyard where Ivy was demanding to try out a tranquiliser gun.

Barb handed her a net. "Can't let untrained civilians loose with darts. In line everyone."

I fell in behind a disappointed Ivy, but despite Aunt Hildegarde's orders, I wasn't going to drop my suspicions simply because she'd told me to. Aunt Hildegarde could keep a tight eye on me, but I was part of a team. Trying to look as if I wasn't saying anything and keeping my lips as still as possible, I hissed in Ivy's ear.

"Ivy. Pretend I'm not talking to you. Listen, I need your help. I've got a bad vibe about OPSA."

Ivy's shoulders straightened but she kept quiet.

Knowing I had her full attention, I carried on. "I want you to do a search on them. I can't because when I told Aunt Hildegarde, she got all stroppy and told me to drop it." I glanced over at my aunt who was watching hawk like from a distance. "See, she's keeping tabs on me."

Ivy wriggled with excitement. "Ooh, covert operation; I like it. Leave it to me. Play along so we fool everyone." Whipping round she whacked me with her net. "You use it!" she bellowed. "And don't blame me when you end up wearing it." Ivy next flounced over to Barb, passing her brothers who took a quick step back. "If I can't have a dart gun then I'm not coming," she said, nose in the air.

Folding her arms, she flopped cross-legged onto the ground.

"Leave her," said Aunt Hildegarde striding ahead. "We don't have time for deserters."

Ivy was spot on about the Gremlin. It didn't intend to come quietly. It drew up a battle line in the kitchen, where it catapulted from wall to wall chucking every appliance it could lay its tentacles on.

"OUCH!" A frying pan frisbeed through the air, smacking Bonzo's head. "You little..." he let fire with his gun, riddling the room with tranquiliser darts. The Gremlin sprang this way and that, but eventually made a tactical error which found it cornered against the fridge. Seizing the opportunity, Barb leapt forward and threw a weighted net over it. The team then filled it with enough sedative to knock out an army. Even so, the Gremlin fought to the last. It took a good ten minutes before it keeled over.

"How is it so strong?" Suze gasped, exhausted. "It's like a secret military experiment."

Old Smokey wasn't any easier. He'd decided that he didn't like OPSA. At first, he tried his fire and smoke routine. Until Phil blasted the contents of a mega-strength fire extinguisher down his throat. The Dragon flopped onto his haunches, foam dripping from his jaws and treated Phil to an evil rumble. Phil hugged the fire extinguisher tightly, but he needn't have worried. Instead of fire, Old Smokey coughed, burped and produced a weak dribble of steam. He observed this first in disbelief and then rip-roaring rage. His ears slapped back flat against his skull, his top lip twisted into an angry curl and every scale on his body rippled like a giant, rumbling tidal wave.

Hissing, the Dragon's spiky tail, attempting to whip Phil (plus anyone in the way) off his feet. We all jumped back as he made a second circuit this time slicing through the heel of Aunt Hildegarde's shoe.

"I think we should find Ivy," Calvin panted as Old Smokey took another swipe, this time almost taking off Joss's head. "We need one of her distracting techniques."

"I'll go," Aunt Hildegarde said. "I'm too old for this kind of exercise." She hurried off. As it was, the problem resolved itself without Ivy's intervention. In the excitement, Old Smokey tripped over his own feet. Whilst he was flat on his back, legs pointed up at the ceiling, Barb fired a volley of darts into his flank. The Dragon's head shot up. Wearing an indignant scowl that slowly changed into a woozy grin, he fell back onto the floor with a thud. A steady, rhythmic snoring filled the air.

"Ah, good. You've managed," a relieved Aunt Hildegarde re-appeared. "Ivy's not here. She insisted on cycling to the village for cakes."

This puzzled the twins. Me too. I'd managed to inform them of the real reason why Ivy had stayed behind. Maybe she was still investigating OPSA and had fed Aunt Hildegarde an excuse. She could be hiding somewhere finishing her task. Or alternatively, she'd found that my suspicions about OPSA were wrong and really had gone off to buy cakes.

"That's not like Ivy. Are you sure?" Calvin said.

Aunt Hildegarde gave an impatient snort. "Yes. So let's stay focused on what *we're* doing. It's time to start loading up the Monsters."

This included Mr Worthington who remained determined to break out of the trunk. Ignoring the muffled banging, Phil and Suze pushed the chest deeper inside the truck, next to Old Smokey's cage. From the sound of his restless, angry snores, the Dragon wasn't having sweet dreams. Barb cast an anxious frown as Phil padlocked the truck's rear doors.

"We should really get moving," she said. "Where's Lady Withershins?"

"I'm here!" Aunt Hildegarde bustled up, struggling under the weight of several pieces of large baggage, bursting with all the things she'd been wearing when she'd arrived. She dropped her luggage on the floor, narrowly missing my toes. "I'm coming with you."

"What?" I said, hopping out of the way. "Why?"

"I have to see the Monsters settled into their new homes." Aunt Hildegarde heaved up a bag and swung it at Bonzo. "Load these into one of the trucks, there's a good chap." Satisfied that he was doing as she said, Aunt Hildegarde resumed talking to me. "The Monsters are bound to be confused and Fitz will be terribly upset if I don't go along to see them settle in." She smiled at Barb. "You don't mind if I come along for the ride, do you?"

Old Smokey rumbled again.

Barb shuddered. "Feel free. The more the merrier."

"But what about me?" I said to Aunt Hildegarde.

"You'll survive." Aunt Hildegarde patted me on the head like I was an endearing but somewhat problematic puppy. "I'll call you later." She swung herself up into the cab of the nearest truck. Barb leapt in at the driver's side and started up the engine. The last we saw of Aunt Hildegarde was her skinny arm waving out of the window as the trucks grumbled off down the drive.

"Wonder where Ivy is," Joss said as we wandered back inside the house.

"Call her," I suggested.

But almost immediately, Joss's mobile rang. He glanced at the screen. "It's Ivy. Hello? What's that? Who is this?" The line went dead. Joss frowned. "Weird. It was Ivy's number, but it didn't sound like her. More like somebody who can't speak English."

"Call back," Calvin suggested. "Maybe Ivy's lost her phone, and someone's found it."

Joss pressed the call back button. From somewhere in the house came the muffled but definite sound of ringing.

I frowned. "Sounds like it's coming from upstairs."

The ringing led us to the first floor and a locked laundry cupboard where Glenda kept the towels. The ringing was definitely from behind the door. I flicked back the bolt. The door swung open. Inside, the phone lay on the bottom shelf. It wasn't alone. Crammed in with the laundry was Ivy, bound from neck to toe in a thick rope. A gag covered her mouth. She reminded me of an irked moth trying to escape from its cocoon. My mouth fell open. Ivy's brothers were less fazed.

Calvin picked up his sister's mobile and inspected it. "Hey," she pressed speed dial with her toe." He looked at Ivy who was mumbling something through her gag. "I'm impressed. What are you trying to say?" He leant forward and dragged the gag down.

Ivy gave her brother a cold glower. "I *said*, what took you so long?" She switched her attention to me. "You were right to be suspicious about OPSA, Kade. There's no animal rights group by that name. It's a removal company who've never heard of Barb and her team. I was talking to the owner – Clive hasn't paid them – when your auntie coshed me. Next thing I knew I was trussed up and locked in here."

"How come she let you keep the phone?" Joss asked her.

"Duh! Do I look like she thought I could use it?" Ivy said.

"But you did," Joss pointed out.

Ivy looked smug. "Yes, she put it there to taunt me. She didn't realise how clever I am." Her preening wilted. "Sir Fitz really rates her. He's going to be ever so disappointed when he finds out that she's an evil old trout. She's left me with a massive headache too."

"Shall I get you an ice-pack?" I asked, feeling responsible.

Ivy laid an accusing glare on her brothers. "I'm replacing you with Kade. He's the only person who's offered me any sympathy. You're rubbish big brothers."

"Stop being sassy," Joss said, bending down to examine his sister's ropes.

Calvin gave me an apologetic grimace. "We'd better tell your uncle the bad news."

"We should do it in person," I sighed. "It's not the kind of news to deliver by phone."

"First, we need to get these ropes off Ivy," Joss said. "Which isn't going to be easy. Your aunt must have been on a rope tying course, Kade. This job calls for scissors." He and Calvin headed off to find some.

There was a heavy **thud!** Ivy, fidgeting away inside her bonds tumbled onto the floor.

"I've been following this podcast series on escapology," she explained. "Although to be honest, I was having trouble with the technique. But falling off the shelf seems to have helped..." She gave one last shake. "Ta daaa!" The rope collapsed around her. Ivy stood up with a satisfied grin. "Let's go find my brothers." She skipped off, singing.

I caught up with her by Aunt Hildegarde's room. The door hung open on the big mess inside. Aunt

Hildegarde's packing had been of the smash and grab style. What she hadn't swept into bags she'd left spilt over the floor or dangling from the open wardrobe and chest of drawers. Her exit had been so fast and chaotic (no doubt because of Ivy) that it was a wonder she'd had enough time to cover her tracks. Had she had enough time? It was possible that in her rush, Aunt Hildegarde might have overlooked something that would give us a clue as to what she was up to. Or where she was headed.

"Ivy, stop," I said. "We're going to search Aunt Hildegarde's room."

Ivy reversed direction. "What for?"

I told her.

"Doubtful, but worth a try." Ivy darted into the room, heading for a pile of abandoned hats. "I'll start with these. Why don't you take the drawers?"

Both searches revealed nothing. The wardrobe proved equally disappointing. The sole place left to investigate was under the bed, which was so huge that its underside resembled a huge, dark cave.

"Silly to leave it out," I said.

Dropping onto our hands and knees, we peered into the gloom. The space underneath was almost a room itself.

"There's nothing," Ivy said, disappointed.

"Let's crawl through in case," I said, scuttling in combat style with Ivy close behind. All we came across were two odd socks.

I was about to give up when my attention was caught by a strip of narrow, brown material poking out from under the door. Aunt Hildegarde had left it shoved so far back that it almost touched the bedroom wall. I pointed this out to Ivy, annoyed with myself for having missed it.

"Don't kick yourself," said Ivy. "I didn't notice it either. After all, it's the same colour as the floorboards."

The strip turned out to be the tag end of a zip. This, as we discovered, belonged to a soft, smallish toiletries bag. I tipped the contents onto the floor. Out fell a tub of stage makeup thick enough to cover the cracks in a wall, a wig matching Aunt Hildegarde's hairstyle, a passport, a notepad, and (I recognised the names) the document from the box.

"There's no way Aunt Hildegarde left this bag behind on purpose," I said.

"Do you think she'll come back for it?" Ivy clicked her knuckles menacingly.

"Not unless she's stupid," I said, picking up the document. With no Barb to stop me this time, I read the whole thing. At the end, I put it down and sat in silence.

"What does it say?" Ivy peered over my arm. I handed her the piece of paper and picked up the notepad. What I read inside didn't make me feel any better. Mutely, I gave that over to Ivy too. Her pupils grew two sizes larger as she scanned the first page. Neither of us needed to speak. Our gaze met for a brief second. Then, together, without saying a word, we shoved everything back into the bag, scrambled to our feet, and fell out of the room. That's when the silence collapsed.

"Calvin! Joss! Calvin!" "Joss! Joss! *Caaal*vin!" Ivy and I yelled together and over each other. The twins were already on their way. We collided at the bottom of the staircase.

"Look at this!" I waved the bag at Joss and Calvin. "Ivy and I searched Aunt Hildegarde's room. Look what we've found." I yanked out the makeup and wig. "The wig must be a spare because Aunt Hildegarde – or who we *thought* was Aunt Hildegarde – definitely had all their hair when they left. And wait, that's not all." I produced the passport.

Joss snatched it. "Withershins, Clive, Percival, Horace," he read out, flashing the photo at Calvin. He pointed at a portrait of the real Hildegarde hanging on the wall. "You have to admit there's a strong twin-like resemblance." (Along with the long, thin, bony features, Clive and Hildegarde had the same moustache.)

"And there's these." From the bag I produced the letter and notepad. "This is a bill from the truck company made out to Clive for the hire of two of their vehicles; and the other contains a list of everyone he owes money to. Their names are balanced against all the people and companies queuing up to buy the Monsters. He's solved his debt problem and we've been had."

Joss rubbed his chin. "It's going to be a big shock to Sir Fitz that he's been tricked. I guess we should tell Victor to call off the chase. No point in him cruising around now."

"What about the T.V crew?" Calvin said. "They'll come back with him."

I leant gloomily against the bannister. "So what? We've lost the Monsters."

Uncle Fitz echoed this statement a short time later, when we stood in front of him.

"So no more Monsters," he said, his voice flat and empty. "Clive's won. The dear creatures who relied on me for protection have been taken to goodness knows where. I've failed them. How could I have been so easily *deceived?*"

"It's not your fault, Fitz." Huddle gave Uncle Fitz's shoulder a comforting pat. "You did your best. They're twins after all, and it was always difficult to tell them apart. Unless Hildegarde was wearing a dress."

Uncle Fitz blew his nose on his handkerchief. "Poor

Gremlin. Eric, Clive tricked him you know into raiding the village. It knows my brother so it wouldn't have been afraid. The poor creature's not a good judge of character." He gave a shuddering sob. "My little Gremlin's probably cowering away in a cage awaiting vivisection. It'll be terrified."

"There must be something we can do," said Joss.

"There is," I said. Ever since the discovery that Aunt Hildegarde was Clive, my brain had been working nonstop. "We're going to find the Monsters and catch Clive too. But first, I need to know what's happening with Angel and Victor."

"Do you mean that ghastly TV woman?" Uncle Fitz fizzed with annoyance. "She came to the station wanting to interview me."

Huddle's nostrils flared. "I wouldn't let her in, so she climbed through the window."

"Yes, which is a good example of how nothing stops her," I said. "If we can get Angel on side with the promise of a good story then I think she'd help us find the Monsters."

"And what story's that?" Calvin asked.

I smiled. "The capture of Clive Withershins: internationally wanted criminal for fraud and theft. I read online that Angel once laid out an investigative journalist for calling her a joke, so rubbing Clive's capture in his face will be a nice follow up to the black eye she gave him."

Uncle Fitz beamed. "Brilliant! Instead of the Monsters we give her a monster scoop."

"You mean we bribe her with Clive, so she keeps her mouth shut about Grosse Manor," Ivy said. "How do we know that she won't demand both stories?"

"Because we'll be as tough as she is," I said. "We won't

146

let her bully us. That way we should be able to come to an agreement."

You could see the hope spilling out from Uncle Fitz. "Really? Is it possible?"

"Leave it to me." I hit Victor's number on my phone. "Victor? It's Kade. How far from home are you and is Angel still on your tail? Good. Stop the car and invite her to a meeting." There was some frenzied talk back from Victor.

"Trust me, Victor," I said, giving the thumbs up to Uncle Fitz. "I know what I'm doing."

Chapter 11

An Angel in Disguise

"How long can Victor take?" Ivy grumbled, shifting from knee to knee on the library window seat. "Even Great Aunt Ida would've arrived by now and she's been dead for ten years."

"Shh," I said, pointing at Calvin who was walking up

and down the room, absorbed in what was written on the sheet of paper he clutched in his hand. "Don't disturb him. He's practising his script."

Calvin's lips moved soundlessly, as he went over and over the list of points to be introduced at the meeting. I'd decided that he should be our spokesperson due to his school council experience. (Good leadership includes knowing when to delegate.)

"Maybe we've got Angel all wrong," Joss put in, rearranging a selection of Glenda's homemade fruit pies, which we'd put out to offer Angel, hoping they'd sweeten her up. "I mean, on the telly she's an image to keep up. Off screen, she might be dead nice."

"Really?" I said. "We're talking about the same person, aren't we? Angel the stalker?"

"Who's arrived," Ivy announced. "Oh, hold on." She squinted through the glass. "Victor's doing his car door routine."

We made it to the window in time to see Angel fling open the car door and stick out a high heeled foot. Victor, cross that she was breaking his game rules, grabbed hold of her shoe. Angel fought back, but although decrepit looking, Victor's surprisingly strong! Joss elbowed Calvin out of the way to get a better view. Calvin pushed back, which led to a fight. Fortunately, it was over by the time Victor creaked his way into the library.

"Miss Lead Block is here," he announced.

"Miss LeBlanc!" Angel shoved past, ponytail slashing as her sharp, green eyes scoured the room. "So, what's going on? Mr Skinny, here," Angel jerked a thumb at Victor, "promised me 'something of interest' if I got rid of my crew. If I've sent them back to the studios for nothing, I'm going to be really annoyed." She glared. "Who's in charge?"

"Kade. He's Sir Fitz's nephew," Ivy said promptly, pointing a finger at me. Calvin, robbed of his opportunity to show off his skills, muttered something uncomplimentary under his breath about interfering little sisters.

Angel gave me a wintry smile. "Then get talking. I don't have all day." It was clear that the warm, friendly approach wasn't her thing.

I met her cold smile with one of my own. "First, show us we can trust you. Who gave you the Gremlin's photo?"

Angel shrugged. "Sorry, can't say. Confidentiality and so forth."

"Think of it as a trade-off, then," I said. "We won't say you told us."

"Not happening." Angel examined her nails.

"You can have first choice of cakes," Ivy wheedled, waving a jam tart in front of her.

Angel yawned. "Not impressed. Righteo then, two of you have proved terrible at negotiating, so let's try..." Her focus locked on Joss. "What do you have to say, sonny?"

"That he's your number one fan and fancies you like mad!" Ivy announced.

Joss, unamused at this disclosure belted Ivy with a cushion. Ivy retaliated by kicking him on the shin.

Joss clutched his leg. "Owwww! You're the worst sister ever!"

Angel's whole being dripped sour milk. I had a nasty feeling she was about to leave. But she didn't. Instead, she walked over to the window seat and sat down, dropping her smart, designer bag on the floor. "You've got two minutes," she said, arms folded.

"Like I said, we need proof that we can trust you," I repeated. "Or no deal."

Flicking back her fringe Angel considered this. An

unpleasant smile lifted the corners of her lips. "Works for me," she said, "I'll give you 'proof' but remember, *you* asked."

With these words an aching chill crept into the air accompanied by a fine, drifting mist that weaved a misty pathway between everything. Angel's hands danced. Whichever direction she pointed with her long, tapered fingers, the mist and chill followed. I shared an uneasy shiver with the twins. Even Ivy was uncomfortable. Victor just picked his nose.

A long, nerve-wracking quietness descended. I could hear the slow tick tocking of the old, brass carriage clock on the mantelpiece. The horrible thought occurred to me that it was counting in the arrival of something terrible. Unease gnawed at me. Angel, head low, released her ponytail. Her hair flooded down. With one swift, scary swoop, she sprang to her feet, flung back her head and let free a bloodcurdling screech. We all copied. Except Victor. Maybe working for Uncle Fitz had made the surprising unsurprising. Ivy and the twins disappeared behind the sofa cushions. I dived under the coffee table. Angel was an angel no more. She was a nightmare! And *green*. Like a frog. She even had the same bulgy eyes. I recognised that look. I saw it every time Glenda appeared. Angel was a Banshee.

"Pack that howling in now, Maudie O'Riley! Though I see you're calling yourself by another name these days!" A second voice, a good ten decibels higher, split the air. In the doorway, gesticulating with her carpetbag, stood a spitting-mad Glenda, hairpins showering down in a storm of metallic rain. Angel cringed.

Glenda marched up to her, seething. "I saw you from the bus stop. Even with all of that makeup plastered over your mug I knew you. And now you come sauntering in here after all these years without a word."

"Hey, Kade," Calvin hissed as I crawled out from under the table. "Even for a Banshee that was loud. She must be really mad."

Angel stuck out her lip. "That's rich," she said to Glenda, her Trans-Atlantic drawl now unmistakably Irish. "When it's you who's been ignoring me. That's why I took up the Grosse Village story. I thought that if I could get into the Manor for an interview, I'd have a chance of seeing you." Her voice crumbled. "Please, Glenda. You're my big sister..."

"Oh, so you remember?" Glenda, bony arms folded, quivered with fury. Her wrath next descended on us, anger dancing down her long nose. "I rushed back after seeing Victor driving along with her ladyship; her, my little sister who ran off from our lovely Irish Bog breaking our dear Mammy and Daddy's hearts. The neighbours never let up about it. She deserves a good drubbing for what she did!" She drew in a long, hissing breath as she took in the fruit pies. "*And* you're giving her my *baking!*"

"But I wanted the bright city lights and a career as a TV News Reporter," Angel protested. "The gassy marshes weren't for me. I needed to go and live my dream."

"The marshes were fine enough for every other Banshee, Miss Too-Good-For-Us -All," Glenda snapped. "No doubt that's why you never got in touch, Miss Posh-Knickers."

"I did!" Angel protested. "But my letters came back marked 'Not At This Address.'"

"Mammy and Daddy had to move bogs after the shame you caused," Glenda sniffed. "And my fiancé jilted me for having a wayward colleen as a sister. I was practically going mad from stress before Sir Fitz gave me a home." Glenda sniffed again. "Which leads me to ask how you knew I was here?"

"Destiny," Angel said. "I was filming an *'Is it Real'* special in Florida searching for a Skunk Ape said to be stalking the everglades and met a Mermaid who told me about this place. Sir Fitz had treated her for a water phobia..."

A sudden flashback rocketed through my head in which an anti-aqua Mermaid howling out, *"Abandon ship!"* floundered in the fountain. "This Mermaid. Was she American?"

Angel paused, surprised. "Yes, she was. How did you know? Oh, you must be the boy she mentioned. It was the Mermaid who gave me the photo I used on my show. She said she'd taken it as evidence after Sir Fitz's kleptomaniac Gremlin nicked her official Miami Marlins baseball cap." She switched back to Glenda. "She also said that an Irish Banshee worked here who matched your description and gave me the manor's landline number, but you wouldn't speak to me. I tried the email address, but I got blocked and I couldn't find any social media accounts."

"I didn't believe it was you," Glenda snorted. "I talked it over with Sir Fitz and we agreed that it was another of his brother's cons. It was a typical Clive tactic."

"But I wrote too," Angel objected. "Loads of times."

"The dog usually eats the mail," I put in, much to Glenda's annoyance.

Angel was unconvinced. "Pardon my scepticism, but that's hard to believe."

"Like your show," I muttered under my breath.

"Back off, kid." Angel had overheard. "You know zilch

about my show, which I do, by the way, for the benefit of the misunderstood Monster population."

"Oh, I get it. You make sure that anybody claiming they've seen a Monster ends up looking such a wally that they never do it again," Joss whooped, grinning at her. "High five!"

"Precisely." Angel ignored Joss's hand. "I've a one hundred per cent success rate."

Ivy, who'd been examining Angel, interrupted. "You know, you and Glenda are the same shade of stagnant pondweed."

"Yes," Glenda said, preening. "Our Banshee clan is famous for it."

Angel, sensing a softening in Glenda, clutched her sister's sleeve. "What can I do to prove I'm sorry? There must be *something*."

Glenda's face snapped shut again.

"Actually," I said, jumping in before Glenda could tell Angel to shove it. "There is."

After hearing the whole story, Angel sat back. "I *think* I can help," she said, twisting a strand of hair around her finger and gazing at the ceiling. "But I'll need to make some calls. Is there a room I can work from?"

"You can use the dining room," Glenda said. "I should chuck you out the front door but if you're going to help, you can stay." She led her sister out of the room.

Having brought Angel on side, the next item on my to-do list was getting Uncle Fitz home. He'd stayed at the station. Huddle had convinced him it was necessary.

"Don't want Clive alerted by any sudden changes to our routine," he'd said. When I'd pointed out that Clive was long gone Huddle had dug his heels in again, insisting that more than likely Clive still had someone keeping tabs on Uncle Fitz. What he really meant was that he wanted to keep his stupid plan alive and kicking.

However, now that we had Angel on board, I'd devised a cunning plot to thwart Huddle. I rang Uncle Fitz, and after revealing Angel's identity substituted the 'thought' she could help for 'definitely' could help. Uncle Fitz had his suitcase packed in nano seconds.

"Eric's going to be very disappointed," Uncle Fitz said. "It'll be another of his crime-catching capers that's failed. I'll have to think of something to soften the blow."

The 'something' turned out to be a promise to Huddle that he could have all the credit for Clive's capture, which made him very happy, although Ivy grumbled about it. Meanwhile, Angel had calculated how far OPSA could've travelled in each direction and had highlighted this on her tablet.

"I've contacts living as humans in each of these zones," she said. "And I've sent out a group message... Hold on; that's Oscar the Ogre messaging back. Oh, shame. He can't help."

"So, Angel's not an exception to Monsters living ordinary lives," I asked Uncle Fitz, as I watched the Banshee working away.

"For certain types, no" Uncle Fitz explained. "With make-up, bit of dentistry, and a large collection of hats, they can blend in quite easily."

"Absolutely," Glenda agreed. "Take Angel." (Having gone by this name for years, she'd asked us to carry on using it. Besides, 'Maudie' wasn't a very glamorous name for a T.V. celebrity.) "Although of course she has a real talent for it."

"You've changed your tune. Not so long ago you were calling her names," I said.

Glenda shrugged. "I'm a Banshee. You can't expect me to give up a grudge without putting on a bit of a show." She stopped as Angel leapt up, waving her phone.

"YES!"

Uncle Fitz, new to the velocity of the presenter's screams, spilt his cup of tea.

"We have a lead," Angel said, grinning. "A friend of mine was out exercising his winged horse over a small, abandoned airfield about fifty miles away and says he saw two trucks fitting the description parked outside an old hangar. He's messaging me the directions."

Uncle Fitz spilt his tea for the second time. "Call Victor to get the car before Clive takes my precious Monsters elsewhere!" Uncle Fitz almost took off into space in his hurry to leave.

"Stop!" Joss called after him. "We don't have a plan for rescuing the Monsters yet."

Uncle Fitz stopped. He deflated like a punctured tyre. "You're right."

"You both are," I said. "We need to get to the airfield before Clive moves the Monsters *and* we need a rescue plan. So, let's get in the car and think something up on the way."

Angel took charge of the driving. Victor was too slow. Uncle Fitz raised no objection to this but did insist on keeping his promise to Huddle who was following with Joe in their police car.

"I promised him," Uncle Fitz said when Ivy complained for the zillionth time, "and he's not coming to the airfield until we've rescued the Monsters. He and Joe have booked themselves into a nice little B&B about ten minutes away. Besides, only the police have the power to legally arrest someone," Uncle Fitz added, seeing that Ivy remained unconvinced.

"We could do a citizen's arrest," Ivy countered.

"If Huddle doesn't show for some reason, then you can help with that," Joss consoled her from the front passenger seat.

"Is Joss sitting there to be next to Angel?" I whispered to Calvin across the pulldown table.

Calvin, sandwiched between his sister and Glenda, shook his head. "No, he gets carsick. He's gone off Angel since she snubbed his High Five."

"Let's go over things again," I said. Our plan was short but hopefully effective. It read:

- **Park in a good surveillance area.**
  (Angel's mate had told us about a useful spot that offered a great view of the airfield.)
- **Ivy (following my radioed instructions) would sneak up to the hangar, suss out the situation and report back.** (Ivy was the fastest and meanest should any nastiness occur.)
- **From the gathered information, set a time to raid the hangar.**
- **Call Huddle and Joe to come and arrest Clive, Mr Worthington, and OPSA.**

"Good job, Kade. Nice and simple, bound to work," said Uncle Fitz with satisfaction.

I crossed my fingers.

Afternoon gave way to early and then late evening as the car purred on. It took a long time. If there'd been a motorway, we'd have arrived at the airfield double quick, but Cornwall went in for long and picturesque roads that took hours to get anywhere.

Eventually, Angel pulled into a side road. "Here we are," she said, applying the brakes. The car's headlights captured the outlines of a thick huddle of dark, creepy trees. Closer inspection also revealed stinging nettles, litter and the smell of stray cats.

"How nice. Not," Calvin said. "This whole place stinks. Some campsite."

"I think it's lovely," Glenda said, adjusting her veil. "There's even a stream."

"That's not a stream." Angel poked her head over her sister's shoulder. "It's not even a ditch!"

Glenda threw her a shirty look. "I'm trying to make the best of it."

"We didn't choose the spot for glamping. We chose it because we can't be *seen*," I said.

Ivy, making a reconnaissance of the area with a pair of night-time binoculars, surveyed the airfield. "I can see the trucks. They're empty. And there's a light coming from the hangar. Nobody outside though."

I swiped the binoculars from her. "Good. Get out there and do your job. Have you got your stuff?"

Ivy huffed at the question. "Of course I have. I'm a Girl Scout; I'm always prepared."

"Then get your headphones on so we can keep in contact," I said, putting on my own set. I tested the mic.

"And be careful," Calvin added. "We're not explaining to Mum how you broke your neck body-sledging down a hill."

So of course, Ivy took the slope as fast as possible, landing in a bramble bush. The resulting yelp echoed through the headphones.

"There you go, never listens," an exasperated Calvin said.

Luckily, apart from a few scratches, Ivy was fine. She scrambled free, brushed herself down and darted across the runway between piles of discarded junk.

I waited until she'd reached the hangar and then instructed her through the mic. "Go around the side, out of sight of the front door."

"Roger that," Ivy hissed cheerfully back.

I followed her progress through the binoculars. The building wasn't in state-of-the-art condition. It was dented and bruised with a corrugated roof like the peel of an old, shrivelled apple. The two windows on that side were high up and so encrusted with years of filth that they looked as if someone had given them a pair of black eyes. Short of going in, which of course was out of the question, I couldn't think of anyway that Ivy could discover anything unless she climbed up. I spoke into the mic again.

"Move to strategy two."

"Ten four," Ivy chirped back. From her belt bag, she drew out a set of hand and knee pads and slipped them on. Taking three counted steps backwards, she then flung herself forwards again and hit the wall, sticking to it like a gecko. Slowly, Ivy suckered her way up. Excited, the twins and I exchanged triumphant High Fives. The pads were further examples of Ben's genius handiwork.

Inching up the gritty, corroded wall, Ivy didn't stop until she came level with one of the grimy windows.

Using its ledge as an elbow prop, she scrubbed at the dirty glass with her sleeve. Unfortunately, Ivy didn't appear to have thought this manoeuvre through. She slipped in a rotation of one hundred-and-eighty degrees, saved from death by the strong suction of her kneepads. The twins clutched each other as their little sister dangled upside-down about four and a half metres above the ground.

"If she kills herself, Mum'll kill us!" Calvin moaned. He and his brother buried their heads in each other's shoulder in order to blank out the sight of Ivy hanging by her knees. Uncle Fitz paled whilst the two Banshees began keening a death dirge. I thought fast and hard.

"Ivy," I said, speaking clearly and firmly into the mic. "Slam your hands against the wall and rotate until you're facing upwards again. Don't be scared."

As if she would be. Ivy gave a cheery thumbs up and complied, crawling round like the hand on a clock ticking away the seconds.

"You can look now," I told her brothers. "She's fine."

"Thank goodness." A frightened Uncle Fitz wiped the sweat from his forehead although the Banshees looked slightly disappointed at their musical soiree being cancelled.

"I'd already thought up an extra verse," Angel said.

Ivy was now peering through the window. After a couple of minutes, she began a more careful descent. However, once on the ground, instead of coming back, she made for the trucks. Something which was *not* in our plan.

"Ivy!" I almost yelled into the mic. "What are you doing? Come *back*."

Ivy's voice threaded its way into my ears. "I'm going to check the trucks. The windows are open. I won't be a sec."

Ignoring my furious instructions to retreat, Ivy swung up onto the steps of the first truck and stuck her head through the cab's open window, wriggling her upper body through.

"What's she doing?" Joss snatched the binoculars from me.

"No idea, she's not responding," I said, as Ivy's lower body surfed the air like a demented dolphin. She gave a last determined kick and tumbled free, landing hard on her rear.

"That must've hurt," Joss said from behind the binoculars.

But Ivy appeared to have a rubber behind. She bounced to her feet and bounded off towards the other truck. Her voice babbled through the headphones into my ears.

"Be quick," I answered reluctantly, ignoring everybody's puzzled looks.

"What did she say?" Joss demanded.

"I'll tell you in a sec. I need to keep close watch." I grabbed the binoculars back.

"She's found something." Angel sounded impressed. "She's a risk-taker. Good for her. Girl Power."

As if to prove the danger, the hangar door swung open. I held my breath. But all that happened was that a hand appeared, tossed out an empty fizzy drink can and then the door slammed shut again. Having finished what she was doing, Ivy slid neatly to the ground and sprinted for the slope. Catching her by the elbows at the top, Calvin and I dragged her into the cover of the trees.

"So?" I said.

Ivy raised a grubby hand. Two sets of truck keys dangled from her fingers. "I guess Clive's not expecting visitors. I get why he's left the cab windows open though.

Those trucks pong!" She tutted at Sir Fitz. "What have you been feeding your Monsters?"

But Uncle Fitz's sole interest was in what was happening to his exotic animals right now. He twisted anxious fingers. "Did you see my Monsters? Are they alright? What's my brother up to?" The questions rattled out.

"Clive's busy working on his tablet and muttering into his phone," Ivy said, sitting up. "But there's no sign of Mr Worthington. Everyone else is lounging about, plugged into their own gadgets and stuffing themselves with burgers. Nobody's taking any notice of the Monsters. Clive must think he's got them all tightly secured and drugged up." She paused. "Actually, the Gremlin's awake and picking the lock on its cage."

"Good, good." Uncle Fitz patted Ivy on the head. "Excellent work."

Ivy preened. "Shall we call Huddle and tell him that we're about to jump Clive and his gang?"

"What if they have guns?" Glenda motioned at herself and Angel. "Bullets won't hurt us. Although the holes would be a bit of a nuisance," she added. "But for humans, gunshots can be fatal. I don't want anything happening to you, Sir Fitz. Nor to you kids either." She dropped her ditch water eyes on the Simpkins and me. "Even though you get on my nerves."

"I didn't see any guns," Ivy said. "Apart from the tranquilliser ones."

"Seeing how many darts they wasted back at the house I wouldn't worry too much about their aim," said Calvin. "Most of their ammo hit the walls."

Uncle Fitz looked pained at this news. But his anxiety over the Manor was about to be replaced by a bigger worry. At that moment, the hangar exploded...

Chapter 12

Help, Get Us Out of Here!

By exploded, I don't mean the hangar blew up. I mean there was an insane eruption of noise.

"Maybe somebody's being tortured." Ivy quivered in excitement. Seizing the binoculars, she trained the lenses onto the hangar. "Aw, I can't see anything. Wait. There's a funny shadow bouncing up and down at the window... Oh, it's the Gremlin."

I wish Ivy had been less descriptive; Uncle Fitz totally freaked out. Every hair on his head stood up like he'd been given an electric shock.

"My gentle creatures! Those fiends are murdering them!" Abandoning our carefully constructed strategy he launched himself down the slope. "Be brave my friends, I'm here!"

Fortunately, living at Grosse Manor had taught me to be flexible when things didn't go to plan. "Okay, let's move, guys," I ordered. "The rescue time's been officially brought forward. Ivy, stay here and call Huddle."

Ivy shoved her nose in the air. "Yeah, like *that's* going to happen." Fast on my heels, she sprang after me in my pursuit of Uncle Fitz, with Joss and Calvin close behind. The two Banshees brought up the rear.

The noise had grown to nuclear proportions. Despite the gimpy leg, the sounds of his critters caterwauling propelled Uncle Fitz as if his shoes had built-in turbo engines. Only Ivy came close to matching his pace.

"Ivy's a sprinter," Joss panted, in answer to my surprised expression. "She trains every day on Dad's treadmill using his outrun an ostrich programme."

Reaching the hangar, Uncle Fitz wrenched open the door. A hairy hand jack-knifed out, seized his jacket, and whisked him inside. Ivy, second to arrive, met the same fate. This gave her brothers new speed.

"Ivy!" Joss bellowed, moving up a gear. "Don't worry, we're coming!"

"Us too!" Kerry called in a show of solidarity. However, two seconds later she twisted her ankle on a tuft of grass and fell into last place along with Glenda who stopped to offer a supporting arm. This meant that the twins and I reached the hangar next.

"We're here, Ivy!" Calvin shouted, opening the door with an impressive karate kick.

Joss followed up with his own martial arts stance. "Come on, Kade," he hollered. "Time to kick butt!"

Not knowing any karate myself, I settled for a rugby charge. We hurtled inside with more speed and determination than shoppers on Black Friday. And then stopped. Ivy hadn't been joking about the Monsters getting free. The area was a disaster movie. Splintered wood, squashed food, ripped up bedding and metal fragments of hinges and locks criss-crossed the floor. Screams and roars bounced off the walls, disappearing within the dark plumes of suffocating smoke billowing from the murky shadows. I so hoped the place wasn't on fire.

"I think the Monsters are getting their own back," Calvin said, fascinated by the scene. He dropped cross-legged onto the floor. "This is like 4D telly."

A Troll scuttled past, dragging Phil by the ankles. Looking back over his shoulder he raised raggedy eyebrows. "And?" he growled. "Any comments?"

I shrugged. "Carry on."

The Troll flashed a wicked grin. "Okey dokey, Boss Man. Cheers."

Phil's eyes reached up and met mine. *"Help!"* His nails raked the ground. I felt a seed of guilt take root. The Monsters had a right to be peeved with OPSA, but I couldn't let them go too far. However, even more important right now was finding Clive and Mr Worthington. Who knew what they were doing? Leaving Calvin, I hurried off.

From behind a stack of boxes, Bonzo scuttled out. He dropped to his knees and flung his arms around my legs. "Let me out of here, I want to go *home,*" he blubbered. "Help me!"

"First, tell me where Clive is," I said, trying and failing to push him off.

Bonzo oozed out fresh tears. "I don't know. Honest."

I believed him. He was too traumatised to lie. I pointed at the cage that had held Old Smokey and which had somehow miraculously remained intact. "The only protection I'm offering is in there."

Bonzo accepted the offer. "I'll take it." He scrabbled

over to the cage. I slammed the door shut behind him, scrambling the combination lock as Glenda strode over.

In his state of shock, Bonzo had started to hallucinate. Grabbing the Banshee's arm through the bars, he pressed his face against her sleeve. "Mummy! You're here! Protect me!"

Glenda bristled. "I'm not your mummy, you horrible human. And don't come near me with that snotty nose. Leave any mess on my clothes and you'll be getting a cleaning bill. Besides," she added, laying him out with a left hook. "You're a bad man."

My eyes went from the fake animal activist, now flat out cold on his back, to Glenda. "Respect!" I said. "Stay close. Your thumping skills may be needed."

"Yah hey, it's Showtime!" Ivy's voice shimmied out from the shadows as she rode full on into the chaos astride a furious Old Smokey (which explained all the smoke). A barking Me, Myself and I gambolled alongside. "I'm modelling myself on Boudicca versus the Romans," she explained. "Like in the telly programme, 'Awful Olden Times'."

Ivy's shrill battle cry struck the air. Pulling Old Smokey's ears, she machine-gunned his head from side to side. The Dragon roared, belching out a stream of hot, arched smoke, his luminous gold-ringed eyes glittered. I could tell he wasn't impressed.

"Want to come up?" Ivy paused in her gunning.

Old Smokey's whole body throbbed out a very pointed 'don't even think about it' vibe.

"No, I'm good," I said. "Besides, I'm after Clive and Mr Worthington."

"Me too." Ivy tugged on Old Smokey's ears. "I think they must be hiding."

"If you find them first, keep them cornered and send

someone to get me; don't let them escape!" I called after her as she disappeared back into the smoke.

"*Save us!*"

Phil's tortured voice begged again for help. The Trolls were trying to ram him headfirst through a crack in the sheet metal wall whilst belting out the lyrics from a movie about seven mining obsessed dwarves.

"This okay?" The Troll gripping Phil's left leg seemed to have forgiven me for trapping him in a barrel. Somehow, he knew my thoughts because he added, "Oh, no worries over that barrel. Yous showed yous was sneaky. That's a well good trait. It's *leadership.*"

Wow, I had *not* expected that.

"In that case, as the boss, I'm ordering you not to kill anyone," I said, taking advantage of the Trolls' new attitude towards me. "And if you don't manage to shove Phil's head through the wall then you're to lock him in with Bonzo. I'll give you the combination." I gestured at the cage whose occupant was beginning to stir.

Close by lurked Amelia, accompanied by Joss. Spotting Bonzo (not yet fully recovered from his experience with Glenda's fist) the Yeti, who was obsessed with soft toys, mistook him for a large rag doll. Squealing, she slid a long arm between the bars, scooped him up in a tight, hairy embrace and started crooning a lullaby. Bonzo, struggling in Amelia's grip, howled.

"Amelia," I said sternly, "put him down."

The Yeti batted her eyelashes and gave an imploring yowl.

I shook my head. "No. This isn't playtime. We need to capture Clive before he escapes. Also, a tall, skinny bloke if you see him. Spread the word." The Monsters of course, didn't know who Mr Worthington was.

Amelia gave a reluctant groan, but much to Bonzo's relief, obeyed. She shuffled off.

"Hey, the Monsters see you as head poncho," Joss said. "They're all doing what you tell them. Your uncle's going to be dead chuffed with you."

"Hey, Kade..." Calvin's voice stopped almost as soon as it began. A large, unexpected missile had crashed down on his head.

"*Ooh, painful!*" Joss winced as his twin hit the ground, moaning.

Mission accomplished the object soared back up. There was a familiar, evil giggle. I froze. I knew that laugh. It was the Gremlin. High in the rafters the hairy horror squatted in a nest of grimy cobwebs, lips twisted in a sneering grin. Relaxing a tentacle, it revealed a very groggy Suze. The thing then slithered across a rafter, hung upside down, and resumed playing yoyos. I leapt back in the nick of time as it threw a tentacle tethered Suze at me. A half-second delay and I'd have been jam. I could see Calvin thinking it was dead unfair that he'd been clobbered whilst I hadn't. The snarling and spitting from the Gremlin showed that it agreed.

Then that stupid dog came along.

WHAM! Off his head with excitement, the mutt hit me with the impact of a double-decker bus. Suze squealed in terror as his heads made a grab for a certain part of her anatomy. (The bit that's important for sitting.) Fortunately for her, he missed. Gabbling and squawking, the Gremlin tugged Suze skywards again.

"Do you think it's time to end this?" Joss asked, heaving Calvin back onto his feet.

I surveyed the scene. The Monsters were seriously enjoying themselves and it wasn't as if anyone was really getting *hurt*. Okay, that was maybe an understatement, but everyone was breathing.

"As long as they're looking for Clive and Mr Worthington, they can have a few more minutes," I said. "Plus, I have to find Uncle Fitz. And look, the Shapeshifter's in trouble. I think all the possibilities for switching form have fried its brain."

The hyperactive Shapeshifter wasn't having a good day. It lay drained on the floor, confused and miserable, uncontrollably morphing into a montage of everything; including how the Gremlin would look if crossed with a Troll. Recognising its situation was serious I jumped to its aid. Close by, the end of a tartan picnic rug poked out from a broken crate. Seizing it by one tasselled edge, I dashed across and threw the rug over the trembling creature, whilst Joss tried to stop its panic attack by encouraging it to breathe into a paper bag.

"That's right, breathe in, breathe out..." he told it.

Shielded from its exhausting possibilities for change, the Shapeshifter gave a final *pop!* and morphed into a clone of my left trainer. Exhausted, the Monster fell asleep. Crisis over, the search for Uncle Fitz began.

The chaos and clamour didn't help. Yells of, *"Help, get me out of here!"* from OPSA as their former captives, Shapeshifter apart (obviously), continued treating them as toys were very distracting. The Banshees didn't get involved. Unless you counted them using Barb as a seat whilst they awarded each Monster a performance score.

"It's like one of those reality programmes, isn't it?" Glenda, enjoying herself addressed her sister. "Where people put each other through awful experiences in order to win big cash prizes."

Angel nodded. "Yes. We could host our own show

called, 'Help, Get Us Out of Here!' because that's what the kidnappers are all yelling."

"I vote for the Trolls and my nephew for good teamwork!" a disembodied voice called. It sounded like Uncle Fitz, but where was he?

"Up here!" Uncle Fitz, perched high on a rafter, beamed down on us all.

I nearly fell over myself. "How did you get there?" I asked, ogling him.

Uncle Fitz was one big soppy smile. "My dear Monsters, having brought me in, were worried that I might get hurt so they popped me up out of harm's way. I did suggest that Ivy joined me, but my friends seemed to think she could take care of herself. Oh look, they're sitting down now in front of the Banshee girls. Bless them, don't they look sweet?"

The Monsters were settled on the floor (Old Smokey minus Ivy who'd vanished) whilst the Banshees explained their scoring system. The creatures gazed at them in hushed expectation.

"Call the police and have us arrested. Please. It's safer." The weak whisper came from Suze. Along with Barb she was now locked in the cage with Bonzo. Her friends seconded the motion. Minus Phil who remained framed in the wall. I frowned. Where were Huddle and Joe?

"Did you call Huddle?" Joss whispered in my ear.

A clanging 'Oh, oh!' of a blunder tolled inside my head. I'd meant to call Huddle when Ivy had refused, but with all the action I'd been distracted.

I made a quick decision. "We'll make a citizen's arrest," I said, recalling Ivy's suggestion on the drive down. "I'll read OPSA their rights. Joss go outside where it's quieter and phone Huddle. Calvin can stand guard over the cage."

"Okey-doke," Joss said cheerfully. He headed for the door.

Calvin nudged me with his elbow. "Which is the real cage? The one on the left or the one on the right? I've been seeing double since Suze landed on my head. Don't want to chase imaginary people if somebody escapes."

This reminded me that Clive and Mr Worthington still hadn't been found. Maybe Uncle Fitz had seen them. After all, from up in the rafters he had an aerial view.

"Uncle Fitz," I called, "what's happened to Clive and Mr Worthington?"

Uncle Fitz gave an apologetic shrug. "Sorry, no idea. According to the Trolls, Clive ran off when the Monsters got loose. Typical; cause trouble but skedaddle when it all backfires."

"Okay," I said. "Then we need to ask the rest of the Monsters if they've seen them."

But the Monsters were focused on Glenda and Angel who'd declared Amelia as winner of their 'Monster's Got Talent' competition. The Trolls weren't happy.

"It's rigged!" a Troll growled. "Banshees is Trollist."

He wasn't alone in being annoyed. An equally fed up Ivy appeared.

"I've not found Clive or Mr Worthington," she said. "I went outside and interrogated Phil. But it doesn't matter how much I say that he's staying stuck in the wall until he comes clean, he says he knows nothing. In fact, he insists that he's never heard of your teacher."

"He's lying," I said.

"That's his story and he's sticking to it," Ivy replied.

"She's right." Joss also reappeared. "And there's no need

to phone. But mind the police car, it's..." The sentence was overtaken by said vehicle crunching through the hangar door. "Here," Joss finished, as the Chief Constable clambered out from behind the wheel. A green-faced Joe followed. I don't think Huddle's stunt driving agreed with him.

By now, all the Monsters were arguing over the Banshees' decision. Listening to it, irritation bubbled up inside me. I scowled. We so didn't need this. Especially at a time when we should be focused on finding Mr Worthington and Clive. Taking a forward I placed myself in the centre of the dispute. It was like having twenty tonnes of fireworks all going off at once the noise was so loud.

"OY, YOU LOT!" I hollered. *"STOP FIGHTING OR FOR THE NEXT WEEK IT'LL BE BREAD AND WATER AT MEALTIMES!"*

This had the desired effect. The Monsters liked a varied diet. Muttering under their breath they sat down.

"Where's Fitz?" Huddle asked.

Joe pointed to the ceiling.

"Don't be ridiculous," the Chief Constable barked at his nephew.

"Actually, old bean, he's correct!" Uncle Fitz gave Huddle a cheery wave.

Huddle's head shot up. His mouth swung open. "Why are you..?" he began but then stopped. Maybe he suspected that the explanation would be lengthy. "Where's Clive and that other crook, Worthington?" he asked instead.

"That's the ten million-dollar question," I answered gloomily.

"Fer ten millyun-dollars, I'll tell yer!" a Troll piped up. The creature's satellite shaped ears had picked up the mention of cash. Waddling over he flashed me a yellow-toothed smile, grimy fingers forming a money-making gesture under my nose.

"Where would I get ten million dollars from?" I said, pushing his hand away.

"Knew it were too good ter be trew," groused the Troll, disappointed.

I grabbed the end of his ratty ponytail as he made to shuffle off. "Wait. If you know anything about where Clive and Mr Worthington are then you need to tell us. It's really important."

The Troll gave a couldn't care less grin. "Nope."

"Then..." I stared about, racking my brain for something that would encourage him to talk and found Ivy. "Ivy will hug you," I said. "Every day." Playing along, Ivy blew the Troll a kiss.

"And as her brother, I'll have to insist that you marry her," Calvin added. "And she'll come and live with you. In your bathroom. In your toilet. Forever. She'll make you wash too."

"No! Not that!" The Troll waved horrified hands. "Honest, I don't know nowt about this Werfington bloke, but Clive put 'imself in that there big trunk. We Trolls thought we might have a nice time laters by buryin' it." He pointed at the huge chest where much earlier on we'd stuffed Mr Worthington.

Huddle strode over to the gigantic box. After a bit of a struggle he managed to slide back the bolt and heave up the heavy lid with a pained groan.

"Is he there?" Uncle Fitz called. "Can you see him? Kade, take a look. Is it Clive?"

Huddle, exhausted from his battle with the bolt, crawled aside to let me pass.

I peered down. Two savage eyes bored into mine. My

mouth dried up like a puddle in the Sahara Desert.

"Umm, no," I said, swallowing the taste of rising hysteria. "Definitely not Clive."

"Bet you're wrong." Ivy elbowed her way through. She took a long, long look and went pale. "Nope," she said. "Not wrong. I take it back. I think it's a vampire," she hissed at her brothers. "Calvin, you had garlic bread for breakfast, breathe on it quick before it gets us."

From out of the trunk rose the long, lean, nightmarish figure of Mr Worthington totally in the style of Count Dracula. Actually, I'd have preferred Count Dracula.

"***What*** have ***you*** kids been ***up to?***" Mr Worthington roared, bellowed and screeched. Suit dishevelled, shirt collar askew and his tie missing, his mood was radioactive. By the law of physics we should have been burnt to a crisp. "***I've*** been ***banging*** and ***shouting*** for ***hours!***"

Uncle Fitz chipped in from the rafters. "That trunk's practically soundproof, old boy. The wood's very thick. Could let fireworks off inside and you'd hardly notice!"

Mr Worthington's attention switched to Uncle Fitz sitting on his perch. "Why are you playing at being a parrot?" he demanded. His gaze moved to his distressed surroundings. "In fact, what have you all been playing at?"

I bristled. Mr Worthington was nothing more than a lowdown crook, yet he was acting as if he had the right to be in charge! I wasn't having it. "Who are you to ask questions?"

"Yes, who are you to ask questions?" Ivy echoed, brave again now she knew the man wasn't a vampire. "We should lock you up with the rest of your gang."

"The rest of my gang? Do you have any idea of who I

am?" The hours spent in that trunk had so not improved Mr Worthington's temper.

"Yeah," I said. "A lying crook."

"*A lying crook? A lying crook??*" The statement hit the air like a humpback whale taking a nosedive. "*I'm an officer from the Police Special Investigations Unit!*" Mr Worthington blasted out the words with more force than a tornado. He almost blew me off my feet. "Read this!" Whipping out an I.D. card from his jacket pocket, he brandished it under my nose.

I read it. Twice. And then a third time in the hopes that this would magically change what it said. It didn't.

"Go on," Mr Worthington poked my shoulder with a bony finger. "Tell this lot what it says. In fact, call Scotland Yard and ask them. The number's on speed dial." He switched the card for his phone. "If I'd been able to get a signal inside that damn box, you'd all be under arrest by now!"

Things so weren't working out as planned. Clearly, my investigative detective skills weren't as good as I'd thought. "It's not our fault," I grumbled. "How were we to know you were a detective? You should've said."

Mr Worthington bounced out of the trunk like a crazed kangaroo. He grabbed my T-shirt, his nose less than a millimetre from mine.

"*I'm* **UNDERCOVER,** *you* **STUPID** *boy!*" he bawled. "*It's all* **PART** *of the* **PLAN!** *That's what I was* **TRYING** *to* **SAY** *when you* **LOCKED** *me in the* **TRUNK!** *I'm absolutely* **FURIOUS WITH YOU!**"

No kidding. The man seriously needed anger management classes.

Mr Worthington gave an unhealthy laugh. "You are in so much trouble, boy. You've wrecked months of police work, falsely imprisoned an officer in a trunk, and assisted a known felon in stealing exotic creatures! I could *throttle* you!"

Huddle, having done nothing so far, decided that perhaps it was time to intervene.

"Don't," he advised Mr Worthington. "It'll damage your career."

"Yes, steady on," Uncle Fitz added. "Apart from the fact that I prefer Kade alive, I don't think you want to upset the Monsters; they're rather attached to him."

Warning murmurs and snarls convinced Mr Worthington that this was true. Especially when the Monsters shuffled closer. Except for two. One was the Gremlin, busy leaping about making cutthroat gestures at me, and the second was the dog. He'd started off well, slinking forward, teeth bared, but had spoilt the effect at the last minute by rolling onto his back inviting a tummy tickle. Mr Worthington growled from deep in his throat but released me.

"Good man!" Uncle Fitz applauded.

I didn't feel quite as chuffed. Apart from half-suffocating me, Mr Worthington had left creases in my T-shirt that you couldn't iron out with a steamroller.

"If you hadn't been snooping around leaving bits of yourself behind, you wouldn't have ended up in the trunk," I muttered.

Mr Worthington's fists tightened. "It's not snooping; it's investigating. It's how secret operations are carried out, sonny, or they wouldn't be secret. He paused. "What do you mean, 'leaving bits of myself behind'?"

"Your glove. I found it under a bush after the Gremlin first went missing," I said. "It was exactly like the ones I saw in your briefcase at school."

"You mean these?" Mr Worthington produced a pair of monogrammed gloves from his pocket. "Unless I have a third hand that I don't know about, I'm not missing any glove."

"But... But..." I stared at the glove with horrified fascination. My mind raced. "But the glove must be yours. Who else has the initials C.W? Oooh. Oh no." Understanding avalanched down like Suze had on Calvin's head.

"Correct. Me!" A crabby voice cut in. "The glove's mine. I lost it climbing down that tree. But who in my family would think of *me*, eh? No one. No. Poor old Clive's not important enough to his relatives for *that*."

Once more, attention was directed at Uncle Fitz's old seafaring trunk. Kneeling up, his hands securely bound together with Mr Worthington's tie, a seething, dishevelled figure eyeballed us all the evils. It was Clive minus the Aunt Hildegarde wig and makeup. I could see why the wig had been necessary. You'd find more hair on a tortoise.

"CLIVE!" It was Uncle Fitz huffing and puffing now. "Somebody fetch a ladder!"

Old Smokey shuffled over. Uncle Fitz swung his legs either side of the Dragon's long neck and slid down He gestured at the untidy figure surfacing from the trunk.

"Clive," he repeated, this time with total disgust.

His brother made a noise that showed he felt the same way.

"Clive climbed in planning to wait until the whole mess was over and then run," Mr Worthington said. "He didn't know the trunk was already occupied."

"You needn't have used me as a mattress though; I have rights," Clive grumbled as Huddle swapped the tie for handcuffs.

"Wait a sec." Angel's forehead puckered up. She pointed at Clive "Say something else."

"Why should I?" Clive snapped.

Angel snapped her fingers. "Got it. Knew I recognised the voice. You're…"

"The person who contacted the studios." Despite being under arrest, Clive managed a smug smirk. "Yes, all part of my plan to get hold of the Monsters."

"But it hasn't worked, has it?" I pointed out.

"Yeah. Loser." Ivy made a big L sign at Clive with her thumb and index finger.

Clive scowled at Uncle Fitz. "This is all your fault, Fitz."

"Mine?" Uncle Fitz ogled his brother. "How is it my fault that you're a criminal?"

Clive cast him such a poisonous glower that it could have withered a rainforest. "Because you're a lousy brother. You sentenced me to a life of crime by turning your back on me. I was penniless when Father disinherited me and gave the Manor and title to you. You were always his soppy, goody two shoes, little favourite"

Uncle Fitz disagreed. "You made your own choices, Clive," he said, pushing Old Smokey's snout away from his hair before it singed. "You chose your path long ago."

"And your cashflow problems are over," I added. "You don't need money in jail."

Mr Worthington nodded. Clive's swagger abandoned him. He went white and then a sickly shade of yellow. I saw him hunt from face to face; human and Monster until finally he stopped at the Gremlin. Clive gave the furball a wheedling smile. The Gremlin gurgled and wriggled its ears.

"Gremley, old chap." Clive's voice was sly, slippery and false. Exactly how the Gremlin liked it. "Won't you help poor Clive? Remember how *happy* you were when I took you on our jolly rampage in Grosse Village? You were so clever using your multiple limbs to steal *and* demolish." He gave the Gremlin another oily smirk. "Use them now. Whisk me up and get us both out of here. We could enjoy a life of crime. Come on now, my little Gremleywemley."

The Gremlin blinked calculatingly. I could see it found Clive's offer tempting. But it was a self-obsessed creature and from its expression thought that Clive's idea had zero chance of working. The Gremlin blew Clive a rude raspberry and leapt onto Uncle Fitz's head. He gave it a fond pat.

"There, there. You're not in trouble. We know that naughty Clive tricked you."

The Gremlin snickered. It reached out and tugged my hair. I jerked away. Uncle Fitz frowned at me. Really, the man was beyond help. But Clive hadn't given up. He targeted Glenda next.

"Will you help me, Glenda? Tell them to release me or you'll deck them with your Banshee singing. After all, I helped you when you were wandering; voiceless and heartsick."

Glenda snorted. "As I recall, you planned on selling me to an Irish American Oil Baron for his heritage collection. Sir Fitz saved me, not you. If things had gone your way, I'd be floating in a giant bottle of formaldehyde somewhere in the depths of Texas. It was pure Irish luck that we stopped at the Manor to pick up a few 'other specimens' as you put it."

"Oh, yes," Clive spat, homing in again on Uncle Fitz. "Dear Saint Fitz. No matter what Hildegarde and I did, we couldn't match you. That's why she ran away to the Himalayas. You drove us to our destinies."

Uncle Fitz gave a weary sigh. "Oh stop it, Clive. You always exaggerate. Hildegarde and I are on the best of terms. We email every week. In fact, she's flying over for Christmas."

Clive sniggered. "I know. I hack your emails. It's how I was able to fool you into believing I was Hildegarde."

Uncle Fitz bristled. "Honestly. Is there no privacy from you? Eric, Detective Worthington, do me a favour and take my brother away. No, hold on. I want him to hear this."

Uncle Fitz put a proud arm around my shoulders. "I don't know what would have happened to my Monsters if it hadn't been for you, Kade. I'm very proud." He aimed his next words at Clive. "My nephew's more of a Worthington than you'll ever be. He deserves a medal." Uncle Fitz hugged me again. "Whatever you want, it's yours."

Not so long ago, I'd have asked for a train ticket back to London. But that was then, not now. Sleepy old Cornwall was deceptive. Life was far more interesting and entertaining here. Besides, I didn't really deserve all this praise. I might not have been responsible for Clive pinching the Gremlin, but I was guilty of being selfish. And there was the whole Mr Worthington thing too. I opened my mouth to confess but then shut it again. After all, everything had worked out for everyone, (apart from Clive) why spoil the moment? Especially when Mr Worthington was quite capable of doing this on his own.

"After all the trouble that boy's caused, he deserves a prison sentence not a medal," Mr Worthington sniped at Uncle Fitz. "He's lucky I'm not hauling him off with Clive."

"Before you do," Angel's voice interrupted as she switched back into her T.V. Investigator persona. "Now that the case is solved, what's the official line on this story..?"

Epilogue

"**...** So, internationally wanted conman, Clive Withershins, is today behind bars along with his gang. Credit goes to a Scotland Yard officer – an undercover detective who can't be named, and Chief Constable Huddle of the Cornish Police Force. Although outnumbered, this fearless officer immobilised the criminals through a cunning plan..."

Angel, promoted by her studio bosses to the role of 'proper' investigative journalist, smiled out from the T.V. in Uncle Fitz's study. This was her first national news broadcast.

"*The Chief Constable has been presented with an award.*" A picture of a proud Eric Huddle with a large medal pinned to his chest filled the screen.

"My little sister." Glenda wiped away a proud tear and blew her nose on her apron. I passed her a tissue.

"It's not fair," Ivy said for the zillionth time. "Huddle didn't arrive until the end. We did all the work."

"A true hero seeks no reward, Ivy. They're satisfied with justice being served," Uncle Fitz answered from his armchair where he sat with the Gremlin snuffling on his knee. It bit his tie in half, lobbing the lower bit my way.

"I'm not satisfied," Ivy said.

Things had worked out for Uncle Fitz, so he was happy. His Monsters were home; he didn't have to worry about Clive anymore; and he'd recently had a very nice visit from the Prime Minister. Mr Worthington had passed the photos of the Monsters to the Government and they'd decided that, as so many exotic species were endangered, Uncle Fitz should keep on with his work and everyone else should keep their noses out. They were even providing funding! Wait until I took over. I'd take some of the dosh and pay Ben Simpkins to build a high-security, Gremlin proof cell. As if reading my mind, the Gremlin unobserved by its doting protector pointed a tentacle at me and curled its remaining ones into fists. I made a mental note to have a squadron of armed guards patrolling its cell twenty-four seven.

"Anyway." Uncle Fitz's voice broke into my thoughts. "I've cleared it with the Government and they're happy for me to use some of the funding to give you all a treat. We're going on holiday."

Holiday? My ears twitched. "Where to?" I shared an excited grin with the twins and Ivy. "Florida? Barbados? A World Cruise?"

"No. Nothing as ordinary as that." Uncle Fitz patted the Gremlin's head. It was now snacking on his shirt buttons. "I'm taking you to the Himalayas to meet the real Hildegarde. She's sent me an email saying that a village near to her monastery has a nest of baby Gremlins, that for some reason the villagers don't want. We're going to collect them. There's one for each of you to take care of on the way back."

The Gremlin climbed up onto Uncle Fitz's head, pulling hideous faces at us.

"It will be lovely for my little friend here to have company of its own kind." Uncle Fitz, deaf to the horrified silence, radiated a beaming happiness. "It can be their adoptive father and teach them all it knows."

Nobody spoke. The twins were rigid with shock. Ivy looked like her worst nightmare had word come true. In the silence, I heard a deep, throaty, evil cackle.

The Gremlin was laughing.

I hated that Gremlin.

ABOUT THE AUTHOR
KD GREAVES

KD Greaves is a former teacher, now tutor, and a logophile! An avid reader from a young age, when she was four, she asked her parents if the family could move to Disneyland because she wanted to live in a "storybook." (An ambition achieved when she grew up and spent several years working as a tour guide in magical, fairy-tale cities such as Venice and Rome.)

Holding a B.A. Hons Degree in History, KD went on to gain a P.G.C.E before working in schools; first as a classroom practitioner and then as a literacy intervention teacher, weaving storytelling into the fabric of her teaching. A great believer that reading for pleasure empowers readers and guides them in finding the voice inside themselves, she has a passion for helping children discover a lifelong love of words.

Parent to three boys, KD's writing career has included a range of well-received stories and playscripts commissioned by the BBC, Channel 4, and Granada Television.

Printed in Great Britain
by Amazon

23915801R00108